# WINK POPPY MIDNIGHT

APRIL GENEVIEVE TUCHOLKE

DIAL BOOKS

DIAL BOOKS
An imprint of Penguin Random House LLC
375 Hudson Street
New York, NY 10014

Copyright © 2016 by April Tucholke

Printed in the United States of America
9-780-8037-4048-8
10 9 8 7 6 5 4 3 2 1

Design by Nancy R. Leo-Kelly
Text set in Aldus Nova

*To all the girls with their heads in the clouds.*

YOU ARE THE HERO OF YOUR OWN STORY.

—Joseph Campbell

# MIDNIGHT

THE FIRST TIME I slept with Poppy, I cried. We were both sixteen, and I'd been in love with her since I was a kid, since I was still reading monster comics and spending too much time practicing sleight-of-hand tricks because I wanted to be a magician.

People say you can't feel real love that young, but I did. For Poppy.

She was the girl next door who fell off her bike and laughed at her bloody knees. She was the neighborhood hero who organized games of Burn the Witch and got everyone to play. She was the high school queen who reached forward one day during math class, grabbed Holly Trueblood's thick, white-blond hair in her fist, and cut it off at the skull while Holly screamed and screamed. All because someone said Holly's hair was prettier than her own.

She was Poppy.

After we slept together, I started crying. Just a little bit, just because my heart was so full, just a couple of small little tears. Poppy shoved me off, stood up, and laughed. It wasn't a nice laugh. It wasn't a *We both lost IT together, how wicked of us, how fantastic, I will always love you because we did this One Big Thing for the first time together* kind of laugh.

No, it was more of a *Is that all it is? And you're crying over it?* kind of laugh.

Poppy slipped her long, white limbs into her pale yellow dress, like milk sliding into melted butter. She was bonier back then, and didn't need to wear a bra. She stood in front of the lamp, facing me, and the ray of light shone right through her thin summer clothes, outlining her sweet girl parts in a way I would think of over and over again afterward, until it drove me insane.

"Midnight, you're going to be the best-looking guy in school by senior year." Poppy leaned her elbows on the windowsill and stared out at the dark. Our high mountain air was thin but clean, and it smelled even better at night. Pine and juniper and earth. The night smells mingled with the smell of jasmine—Poppy dabbed it from a tiny glass bottle in her pocket, each earlobe, each wrist.

"That's why I let you have me first. I wanted to give it to *him*. He's the only boy I'll ever love. But you don't know anything about him, and I'm not going to tell you anything about him."

My heart stopped. Started back up again. *"Poppy."* My voice was weak and whispery and I hated it.

She tapped her fingers on the sill and ignored me.

An owl hooted outside.

Poppy swept her blond hair back behind her shoulder in that gangly, awkward way she still had then. It was completely gone by the time school started up—she was nothing but smooth elegance and cold, precise movements.

"And now no one will be able to say I didn't have taste, Midnight Hunt, even when I was young. You're going to be so beautiful at eighteen that girls will melt just looking at you, your long black lashes, your glossy brown hair, your blue, blue eyes. But I had you first, and you had me first. And it was a good move, on my part. A *brilliant* move."

AND THEN CAME the year of me following Poppy around, my heart full of poetry and bursting with love, and never seeing how little she really cared, no matter how many times I had her in my arms and how many times she laughed at me afterward. No matter how many times she made fun of me in front of her friends. No matter how many times I told her I loved her and she never said it back. Not once. Not even close.

# WINK

EVERY STORY NEEDS a Hero.

Mim read it in my tea leaves the day Midnight moved in next door. She leaned over, pushed my hair out of the way, put her fingers on my chin, and said: "Your story is about to begin, and that boy moving boxes into the slanted old house across the road is the start of it."

And I knew Mim was right about Midnight because the leaves also told her that the big rooster was going to die a bloody death in the night. And sure enough, a fox got him. We found him in the morning, his soft feathers stiff with blood, his body broken on the ground, right next to our red wheelbarrow, like in that one poem.

# POPPY

I FELL IN LOVE with Leaf Bell the day he beat the shit out of DeeDee Ruffler.

She was the biggest bully in school and he was the first and only kid to take her down. I'm a bully too, so you might have thought I'd sympathize with her, but I didn't.

DeeDee was a short, wrong-side-of-the-tracks nobody with a mile-high cruel streak. She had a strong, stupid body and a plain, round face and a mean, grating voice, and she'd tried to fight Leaf before, she'd called him all kinds of things—poor, ginger-haired, skinny, dirty, diseased—and he'd just laughed. But the day she called little seventh grader Fleet Park a *slant-eyed boy-loving Chink*, Fleet started crying, and Leaf snapped. He beat DeeDee into a coma, right there on the school's cement steps, he pounded her head on the concrete, knees pinning her down by the chest, her boobs jiggling, his red hair flying around his lanky shoulders, the snow-capped mountains in the background.

My heart swelled three sizes that day.

DeeDee was never the same after Leaf smashed her head in. I'd read about lobotomies in my Modern Woman's Science class, and that's how she was now: detached, lethargic, useless.

Leaf didn't get into trouble for that fight, he never got in trouble, just like me. Besides, everyone was sick of DeeDee, even the teachers, especially the teachers. She was as mean to them as she was to everyone else.

There was an evil in me too, a cruel streak. I don't know

where it came from and I didn't really want it, no more than I'd want big feet or mousy brown hair or a piggish nose.

But fuck it. If I'd been born with a piggish nose, then I would *own* it, like I own the cruel and the mean.

Leaf was the first to recognize me for what I was. I was gorgeous, even as a kid. I looked like an angel, cherub lips and blushing cheeks and elegant bones and blond halo hair. Everyone loved me and I loved myself and I got my way and did what I wanted and I still left people feeling like they were lucky to know me.

No one thinks they're shallow, ask every last person you know, they'll deny it, but I'm living proof, I get away with murder because I'm pretty.

But Leaf saw right through the pretty, saw straight through it.

I was fourteen when Leaf Bell lobotomized DeeDee on the school steps, and I was fifteen when I followed Leaf home and tried to kiss him in the hayloft. He laughed in my face and told me I was ugly on the inside and left me sitting alone in the hay.

# WINK

EVERY STORY NEEDS a Villain.

The Villain is just as important as the Hero. More important, maybe. I've read a lot of books—some out loud to the Orphans, and some just to myself. And all the books had a Villain. The White Witch. The Wicked Witch. The Gentleman with the Thistledown Hair. Bill Sykes. Sauron. Mr. Hyde. Mrs. Danvers. Iago. Grendel.

I didn't need Mim's tea-reading to learn the Villain of my story. The Villain had blond hair and the Hero's heart on her sleeve. She had teeth and claws and a silver tongue, like the smooth-talking devil in *Ash and Grim*.

# MIDNIGHT

I HAD AN older brother. A half brother. His name was Alabama (to be explained later) and he lived with our mom in Lourmarin, France. My parents weren't divorced. They just didn't live together. My mom wrote historical mysteries, and two years ago, in the middle of a blizzard, she decided she would keep writing historical mysteries, but in France instead of here. My dad sighed, and shrugged, and off she went. And Alabama went with her. He'd always been her favorite anyway, probably because his father was my mother's true love. Alabama's dad was Muscogee and Choctaw. He ran back to Alabama—the state, not the brother—before my brother was even born. Then *my* dad came along, with his big heart and weakness for creatures in need. He married my pregnant mother, and the rest was history.

Until she gypsied herself and my brother off to a land of grapes and cheese last winter, that is.

So my dad sold the dull, spacious, three-bedroom, three-bathroom house I grew up in, and moved us into a five-bedroom, one-bath, crumbling, creaking old house in the country.

Five acres, apple orchard, sparkling, bubbling creek. Just in time for summer.

And I didn't mind. Not a bit.

The house was two miles from town, two miles from Broken Bridge, with its Victorian houses and cobblestone streets and expensive gourmet restaurants and hordes of skiing, snow-bunny tourists in the winter.

And it was two blessed, beautiful miles away from Poppy.

No more soft taps on my window in the middle of the

night from the girl three doors down. No more Poppy laughing as she crawled over my windowsill and into my bed. No more me not knowing whose cologne I smelled all over the front of her shirt.

I was done being a sucker. And this old house, nestled between apple trees and pine trees, in a shadowy, forgotten corner of the mountains . . . it was the first step to my freedom.

My freedom from Poppy.

# POPPY

I WOULD HAVE given it to Leaf the second he asked for it, except he never ever, ever did, so I gave it to Midnight instead.

Midnight and his big droopy eyes, his heart hanging out of his chest, the sighs, the softness, the kisses. I hated him for it, really, really hated him for it, hated hated.

Hated, hated, hated, hated.

My parents still thought I was a virgin. They never discussed sex in front of me, they refused to acknowledge that I'd grown up because they wanted me to be their stupid little angel baby forever, and it made me rage rage *rage* inside, all the time, all the time. I wore the shortest skirts I could find, and the lowest-cut tops, oh, how they squirmed, their eyes scrambling to focus on some part of me that wasn't sexual, so they could keep on thinking of me as they always had.

My parents still gave me dolls as presents, ones that looked like me, blond, with big eyes and puffy red lips. And whenever I saw another box sitting on the kitchen table, wrapped in pink paper with my name on it, I knew I would find myself over at Midnight's window later that night, tap-tap-tapping, wanting to be let in so I could prove to myself how un-angelic I was.

Most men lead lives of quiet desperation. Leaf said that a lot. It was some quote from a tree-hugging hippie who lived a boring life in the woods a million years ago, and Leaf probably thought it would open my eyes and make me wise up and get in touch with my inner deeps, but all it did was make me want to tear off all my clothes and run through the town screaming.

If I was going to lead a life of desperation, then it would be *loud*, not quiet.

# WINK

I watched the Hero as he moved boxes into the old Lucy Rish house. I stood by an apple tree, and I was there a long time before he saw me. I was good at not being seen when I didn't want to be. I'd learned how to be quiet and invisible from reading *Sneaks and Shadows*.

I hadn't shown *Sneaks and Shadows* to my brothers and sisters. I didn't want them learning how to hide in broad daylight. Not yet.

I hoped the Hero would like it in his new house. Lucy hadn't liked it. She'd been a mean, superstitious old woman who called us witches and clutched her rosary whenever she saw us. And she threw apples at the Orphans if they played too close to her lawn. Her husband had been nice, he was always smiling at us from across the road, but he died three years ago. Felix thinks Lucy poisoned him, but I don't know. Old people die all the time without the help of poison.

# MIDNIGHT

I LOOKED UP, and there she was suddenly, standing at the bottom of the front steps, wearing a little green button-down shirt and a pair of baggy brown overalls with huge strawberry buttons on the straps. It was an outfit a kid would wear, not a seventeen-year-old girl. The overalls were dirty and too big for her little body.

Wink was one of the infamous Bell kids. They never seemed to end and who knew how many there really were in the first place.

But now I lived next to them and so maybe I would be able to find out. Maybe that would be my second goal of the summer, like this:

1. Get over Poppy. For good.
2. Count the Bell kids.

In elementary school, Wink Bell had been called Feral Bell behind her back because her hair was messy and her clothes were always kind of dirty. *Feral* was a big word for little kids, which, looking back, makes me think some bitter teacher gave her the nickname first. People still called her Feral sometimes, and she didn't seem to notice really, let alone mind.

All the Bell kids had weird names, just like me and Alabama, and I'd always felt drawn to them for that, if nothing else.

I shifted the box of books I was carrying to my other arm, and stared at Wink. Her red hair curled into long, tight spirals that draped over her thin shoulders and she had freckles on her nose and cheeks and just about everywhere else. Her eyes were big and green and . . . innocent. No one's eyes looked like that anymore. No one my age, at least. Our eyes grew up and stopped believing in magic and started caring about sex. But Feral's . . . they still had a faraway, puzzled, lost-in-an-enchanted-forest gleam to them.

"You look like someone," Wink said.

I put the box of books down on the porch and Wink must have taken that as an invitation, because she walked right up the steps and stood in front of me. Her head barely reached my shoulder.

"You look like someone," she repeated.

People in school thought Wink was strange. Beyond strange. If a person was just a little weird, that person could be made fun of. Maybe they knew too many *Star Wars* quotes, or maybe they talked to themselves, or lived in a one-room mountain shack, or smelled like basement, or did magic tricks in school every chance they got because they wanted to be magicians. These people could be teased. Laughed at. Made to cry. But not Wink. The bullies had given up on Wink and her siblings years ago. The Bells were impossible to ridicule—they were never, ever embarrassed. Or scared. Eventually the bullies got bored and moved on to easier prey.

Wink had an older brother named Leaf. He graduated last year, but when he'd been in school everyone, *everyone*, had been afraid of him. Leaf had calm green eyes and dark red hair, as straight as Wink's was curly. He was tall and lean and you'd never think he'd be able to beat the hell out of anyone. But he did. All the time. He had a temper on him that no one, not even the teachers, took for granted.

Everyone said the Bell kids were witches and weirdoes. And people left them alone. And they seemed to like it that way, for the most part.

So why was Wink standing on my porch right now and staring at me and looking like she wasn't going anywhere?

Wink reached into a pocket of her overalls. It was so deep her whole arm disappeared inside. When she pulled her hand back out, it held a small book. She flipped through it, found what she was looking for, and handed it to me. It was old, and the pages were half falling out. Wink held it open at an illustration of a boy with a sword at his side. The boy was on a hill, facing a dark stone castle, grim-looking mountains in the background. He looked like he was waiting . . . waiting for something to come out and kill him.

"That's Thief," Wink said, pointing one of her short freckled fingers at the boy. "He fights and kills The Thing in the Deep with the sword his father left him." She tapped her fingertip on the page. "See his brown curly hair? And his sad blue eyes? You look like him."

I glanced at the illustration again, and then back at Wink. "Thanks," I said, though I wasn't sure it was a compliment.

She nodded, kind of gravely, and put the book back in her deep pocket. "Have you read *The Thing in the Deep*?"

I shook my head.

"I've read it to the Orphans many times. *The Orphans* is what I call all my sisters and brothers, because there are so many of them and because we don't have a father anymore. We do have a mother, so they're not *real* orphans, but she's always busy reading people's leaves and cards and we're left to ourselves, mostly."

Wink paused.

"That's why you'll see a lot of strange cars in our driveway. A strange car means someone is here, and she's reading their cards."

Wink paused. Again. She was in no hurry.

"Mim read my leaves and she said you and I were going to have a story together. I was wondering if our story was going to be like *The Thing in the Deep*, because you look like Thief."

Wink took a big breath, let it out, put her hands in her pockets, and stopped talking. A breeze floated by and lifted her thick hair off her shoulders. After her long speech, she now seemed content to just let us stand in silence.

I didn't quite know how to talk to Wink yet. That would come later. But I already found her sort of relaxing. The seconds ticked by and I listened to the trickling of the creek down by the apple orchard and the rustling sounds of my dad unpacking inside. I felt my shoulders ease downward and my posture soften. Being with Wink was somehow like being alone, except not, you know, *lonely*.

And eventually I realized that the reason I felt so peaceful was because Wink wasn't taking stock. She wasn't trying to figure out if I was sexy, or cool, or funny, or popular. She just stood in front of me and let me keep on being whoever I really was. And no one had ever done that for me before, except maybe my parents, and Alabama.

"So what happens in the book?" I asked, after a few minutes of breezes and curly hair and overalls and not-judging and soft, peaceful quiet. "What happens to Thief?"

"There's a monster in the shape of a beautiful woman. She kills people. Children, old people, everyone. She tries to kill the girl that Thief loves. He fights the monster, and he kills her, because he's the hero. There is a great victory. And a descent into darkness. There are clues and riddles to solve, and trials of strength and wit. There's redemption, and consequences, and ever after."

I've read a lot of books too. More than I let anyone know, except my dad. I read a lot in the last year especially. My days had been shuffling from class to class, driving all my damn friends away with my mood swings, and my nonstop Poppy-this-and-Poppy-that-spewing, and my love, love, love, love, always my *love* for this blond-haired girl who sometimes held my hand between classes and sometimes kissed me on the lips when people weren't looking, but mostly, mostly ignored me, leaving me following behind, calling her name and her refusing to turn around.

But my nights, the ones where Poppy didn't knock on my window, were spent with my books. I read a lot of science fiction and way more high dragon fantasy than is probably good for a person. I read the classics, like Dickens and *Animal Farm* and *Where the Red Fern Grows*. I even read some historical romance and some murder mysteries and horse-and-gun Westerns. I didn't care. I read it all. Alabama was basketball and cross-country and leaning on things and jumping off things and all the girls liking him. But I was the reader brother who liked to swim in rivers and hike in the rain and sit under the stars but never, ever play organized sports. And I supposed I was all right with this.

Wink and I kept staring at each other. She was running this conversation, and I let her call the shots. She turned, and looked down at the books in the box I'd been carrying, so I got a chance to notice the soft-looking batch of freckles on her inner arms, and how small her nose was, like it belonged on a doll, and her short, stubby, faded-red eyelashes, and her pointed chin.

My dad walked by us at one point, tall, thick brown hair, wire-rimmed glasses, easy, soft stride. He liked to run, when he wasn't reading or selling rare books to people in faraway places, and his running meant he moved like a cat. He reached in and got a lamp from the moving van, strode quietly back, smiled, and carried the lamp inside, letting us get on with our silence.

*"Midnight."*

A girl's voice shredded the breezy stillness. I jerked my head toward the sound.

Poppy.

She was standing at the edge of the woods, on the other side of the lane, at the edge of the Bells' rambling farm.

I guess two miles wasn't far enough after all.

Damn.

Poppy passed by the red barn, the four Bell outbuildings, and their old farmhouse with its red slouchy roof and tall windows with black shutters. She crossed the road that was really just gravel and weeds, wove between our four bright green apple trees, walked up the wooden porch steps, and stood in front of Wink as if she weren't there. She was wearing a white loose dress that still managed to hug her body in a way that whispered *I paid too much for this*. Poppy was the spoiled only child of two busy doctors who raked in money from the snowboarding celebrities-with-a-death-wish that bombarded Broken Bridge every winter. Her house was one of the biggest around, including the endless second homes owned by film stars and aging musicians.

She ran her hand through her hair and smiled at me. "Do you know how long it took me to walk here? I can't believe I bothered."

I didn't look at her. I watched Wink walk down the steps, turn, and go back to her farm across the road without another word, quiet as a nap in the sun.

"My parents won't get me another car until I graduate." Poppy squeezed her perfect lips into a pout, oblivious to Wink's departure, as if she were a ghost. "Just because I took the new Lexus without asking and then totaled it by the bridge. Fuck. They should have expected that."

I ignored her. I stared off at the Bell farmyard, distracted by a bit of green and brown and red that was climbing a ladder attached to the big barn that stood off to the right of the white ramshackle farmhouse.

Wink disappeared into the dark square of the hayloft opening.

I'd known Wink all my life, but really, for all practical purposes, I'd only just met her.

Poppy snapped her fingers in my face, and my eyes clicked back on her. She looked annoyed and beautiful, as usual, but I wasn't really noticing for once. I was wondering what Wink was going to do up in that hayloft. I wondered if she was going to reread *The Thing in the Deep* to the Orphans.

I wondered what it was going to be like, living next to a girl like that instead of a girl like Poppy.

I suddenly wished, with my whole damn heart, that I'd always lived in this old house, across the road from Wink and the Orphans.

"Midnight, Midnight, Midnight . . ."

Poppy was saying my name over and over in the drippy sweet voice that had once set me on fire and now just made me feel cold.

I yanked myself out of the peaceful, surreal feeling that Wink had cast, and finally focused on the girl in front of me. "Go home, Poppy."

Poppy blinked her tart gray eyes. Slowly. She played with the expensive pockets on her expensive dress, and smiled at me—her gentle, sad smile that, with very little effort, she could make seem sincere. "We're not over, Midnight. We're not over until I say we're over."

I couldn't even look at her. The peaceful Wink feeling was gone now, entirely gone. All I felt was anger. And melancholy.

Poppy reached up and put her hand on my cheek. Her eyes hooked into my skin and pulled my face down, toward hers, like a fish on a line.

I fought her. But not nearly as hard as I wanted to.

Poppy was used to getting what she wanted. That was the thing about Poppy.

She won. She always won.

# POPPY

LEAF DIDN'T TALK in school, he didn't stand around and yak about boy things with other stupid boys, none of the Bell kids talked, really, which is one of the things that made them so weird. Leaf was eerie and still and quiet, and he always looked bemused or angry. And when he didn't look bemused or angry, he looked blank and distant and removed, like he wasn't seeing anything or anyone else around him at all.

Bridget Rise was a pants pee-er. Her older brother had been a pants pee-er too. I guess it ran in the family, a genetic pants-peeing gene, like having bad eyesight or dry skin or thin hair, something that evolution should have bred out, Darwin style. The last time Bridget peed her pants was at recess in third grade. Some of the kids called her gross and started throwing dirt at her, little tight handfuls of it that got in her hair and down her shirt.

I might have thrown some of the dirt. I might have given the other kids the idea. Bridget was crying, sobbing, sobbing, and then out of nowhere Leaf was there. He was eleven or twelve, but he had the temper, even then.

He picked Bridget up, soaked jeans and dirt and everything, and carried her into school.

And then he came back outside and kicked the shit out of every last one of us, everyone with dirt on their hands, literally, me included. He shoved my face into the ground, right into the mud I'd been throwing, and told me that if I teased Bridget again he'd break my nose.

He meant it, we all knew he meant it. And when I forgot anyway and called Bridget *The Tinkler* two weeks later at lunchtime, Leaf found me after school, one hand, one punch, that's all it took, my eyes crossing as his fist hit my face, crack, snap, blood, scream.

My nose was still crooked from it. Even my doctor parents couldn't fix it, not perfectly. Midnight said it made me even more beautiful, the tiny imperfection, but he read poetry and his mind was soft, like his heart. I stopped listening to him years ago.

I didn't let Leaf's laughter deter me that day in the hayloft. I was confused because I'd never lost at anything before, but I was high on the challenge, and I wanted to try at something for once, *really* try. That's how I felt, at first.

The day I turned sixteen I walked up to Leaf between classes. I leaned my body against his gray locker, back arched. I was wearing the shortest skirt I owned, the one that made my legs look ten feet long, the one that made Briggs start drooling at Zoe's party the other night, he actually drooled, and had to wipe his mouth with his hand. I'd left my bra sitting on my bed, and I knew my nipples were showing through my black slub T.

"Hi, Leaf," I said, using the low, breathy voice that brought boys to their knees.

And he looked at me. Not with lust, or craving, or greed. He looked at me in the same way I looked at the band nerds in their marching uniforms as they bumbled down the hall carrying their stupid shiny instruments. The same way I looked at the spineless boys in my class with their panting eagerness and pathetic over-confidence and wispy arms and spindly legs.

"Move."

That's all Leaf said. He stood there, tall and skinny and red-haired and barely caring and all he said was *move*.

I never cried, not even as a baby. My parents said it was

because I was such a *sweet little angel*, but my parents are fools. I never cried because there are only two reasons people cry, one is empathy and the other is self-pity, and I never had any of either. I cried over that *move*, though, I cried, cried, cried.

Revenge.

Justice.

Love.

They are the three stories that all other stories are made up of. It's the trifecta. It's like if you're making soup for a bunch of Orphans. You have to start with onions, and celery, and carrots. You cut them up and toss them in and cook them down. Everything that comes after this is just other. Stories are that way too.

I told the Hero about the Orphans, and *The Thing in the Deep.*

I liked his eyes.

# MIDNIGHT

POPPY FOLLOWED ME through my new house, across the creaking hardwood floor, around jumbled-up furniture, under spiderwebs, over boxes, up the stairs, hands sliding over the smooth dark wood of the banister, down the narrow, dark hallway, to the high-ceilinged bedroom that I'd taken as my own, last door on the left.

There weren't sheets on the bed, but the frame and mattress were up. I stepped over two boxes and then moved around the room and opened all the windows. All four had faded yellow curtains that smelled like dust.

I went back to the door and closed it. Dad wouldn't bother me if my door was closed. He respected privacy. Privacy was like gold to him, as in worth-its-weight. He wanted it, and so he gave it to others freely and without question.

I had to push the door shut the last few inches, so it would latch. This house seemed to be leaning on its side, like an old woman with one hand on her hip, and it made everything off kilter. Later on, I would come to like it. Later on I would hear the creaks and moans and feel welcome, and comforted, like the house was speaking to me in its own gasping, rickety voice. I would be able to tell where Dad was, down to which corner of the room, just by the series of pops and shudders and squeaks that echoed down to me like the refrain of a song I knew by heart.

But back then, it was just an old house, two miles away from Poppy, across the road from the Bell farm.

I turned around.

Poppy stood in the dusty sunshine of my bedroom, wearing nothing but a thin white summer dress and the skin she was born in.

How could something so soft and supple and flawless as Poppy's skin hide a heart as black as hers? How could it show none of what was underneath, not one trace?

I'd read *The Picture of Dorian Gray.* I wondered if Poppy had a painting of herself locked in an attic . . . a painting that was growing old and evil and ugly and rotten, while she stayed young and beautiful and rosy-cheeked.

I sat on the bare mattress with a sigh. Poppy crawled into my lap. She kissed my neck. Her hands were on my shoulders, chest, stomach, down down down . . .

"No," I whispered. And then louder. "*No.*"

I picked up Poppy by her hips and moved her onto the bed beside me. Her dress was pushed up to her thighs, and she crossed her naked legs, looked up, and smiled. "So never again? Is that it? You're done with me now? You move out to this rat-hole farmhouse and suddenly it's over?"

I met her eyes. "Yes."

She laughed. She laughed, and it was hard and slick and cold, like chewing on ice. She got up from the bed and went to one of the two big windows on the east wall that faced the road, and the Bell farm.

"You're going to be living next to *her* now." Poppy glanced at me over her shoulder, her eyes mean and sly. "Feral Bell. That should prove interesting for you."

"Don't call her that." I got up off the bed and joined her at the window. I looked past the three lilac bushes, past the old well, past the rope swing on the ancient oak tree, past the pine trees, past the fields of corn on the left that were rented out to a neighboring farm, past the apple orchard, across the road.

Our houses were close, even with the gravel lane between them. I could see everything. I saw chickens running around, following a rooster, and two goats in a white pen, and three kids playing with a dog, and another climbing the ladder of the red barn. I could hear shouts and laughter and crowing and clucking and barking. I could even smell gingerbread in the oven—the dark, sweet, spicy smell drifted right over the road straight to my nose.

It seemed so much nicer over there, in Wink's world. Much,

35

much nicer than being in this empty, foreign bedroom with a red-blooded Poppy.

"Don't call her what? *Feral?* It's better than Wink. Wink is like something from a children's book. *And then Wink and her pink horse, Caramel, rode off to Fairyland on a path made of clouds.*"

Poppy was watching the farm, closely, almost as if she'd forgotten I was there. "Look at all those kids running around. Why should Wink get so many siblings while I have none? Leaf said once that I would have been a better person, if only I'd had a sibling or two. He said I'd be 'less selfish by half.' As if I—"

"Leaf?" I said. "Leaf Bell? You used to know him? People at school said he's down in the Amazon searching for a cure for cancer. They said he sleeps on the ground and eats nothing but nuts and berries and he speaks their Mura language like a local—"

"Shut up." Her eyes were back on mine. "Just shut up, Midnight."

She went to the door, opened it, left.

Came back.

She sidled up to me and put two fingertips on my heart. Pressed.

"You and the Bell girl . . . you looked good together."

I said nothing, waiting for the punch line.

"I mean it, Midnight. You should get to know her better."
She moved her fingers to my cheek, and ran them down, over
my jawbone, across my neck. "Wink is weird and quiet and so
are you. You two should be friends."

I flinched. "What are you up to, Poppy?"

"Nothing. I'm just trying to be a better person. I'm bored
with being mean, bored, bored, bored. So I'm attempting to
improve myself. I'm setting you up with the weird girl across
the road. I want you to be happy."

"No you don't. You don't even know what the word means."

But she just shrugged, and laughed, and left.


# POPPY

I SNUCK OVER to the Bell farm once a few years ago, and just
watched the goings-on from the shadow of the woods. I was
there for a while, and they never even looked in my direction,
not any of them, like I was invisible, like I was a ghost.

I had this idea that I'd catch Leaf off guard, and maybe a
look would pass over his face, fleeting but there, really there,
and then I would know. I would know that he thought of me.

He and Wink were outside with their siblings, they had
a picnic and then played some game with a lot of hooting

and hollering, and he was different with them, so different, especially the pretty brunette sister, he was rowdy and loud and he laughed all the time. I'd never even heard his laugh, not his *real* laugh anyway. And after a while I started feeling bad about myself, standing alone in the woods while they all laughed and played together, and I'm Poppy, I never feel bad about myself, ever, so I went home and never did it again.

The eighth time I followed Leaf to the hayloft, I kissed him with my whole soul, all of me, all the bad parts and the good parts too. I kissed and kissed him, his thin straight nose, his freckled cheeks, his wide bony shoulders, his hard white torso, but his green eyes never even met mine, not once. So I got naked, I thought I would stun him with my stunning beauty, but he only shrugged his shoulders and said I could be the spitting image of Helen of Troy for all he cared, I was still not worth the breath I breathed.

His younger sister called out from somewhere in the yard and he went down to her without another word. I cried while I put my clothes back on, fast, fast, the hay caught up in the creases and scratching me all the way home, but it felt good, like the nuns and their hair shirts, a punishment on the path to redemption.

# WINK

WHEN THE HERO knocked on our old screen door at sunset I thought he was coming to get his fortune told, like everyone else who came to our house.

He came bearing one pink little wildflower in his hand and he gave it to me when I opened the door. I didn't know what to do with it so I just held it in my fist while he stood there looking pleasant and awkward like the ordinary farm boy before destiny knocks and he's forced to pick up the sword and take to the road.

I let him inside and then, before I could change my mind, I asked him if he wanted to go for a walk in the forest.

He looked out the windows at the setting sun, and then said yes anyway.

I planned to take him down the path that went right by the Roman Luck house. The Roman Luck house was full of bad things and sadness and unforgivables, but I wanted to see what would happen.

Midnight waited in our kitchen while I got ready. The Orphans surrounded him, asking him questions he didn't know how to answer, mostly about whether he'd seen the ghost of Lucy Rish yet in his house across the road, and if she threw apples at him or if they fell right through her old ghostly hands. He smiled and didn't seem to mind all their asking.

I put on a green cotton dress, because the tree spirits like green. It had been Mim's dress when she was a girl, and had a white belt. There was only one little hole, in the back, where you could hardly see it.

I forgot to brush my hair before we left, but I did remember to dust my arms and neck with powdered sugar. It made the mosquitoes come at you, but the night was blustery and I wasn't worried. Besides, the unforgivables will feed on you, unless you give them something sweet. It distracts them and they leave you alone. Mostly.

## MIDNIGHT

THE INSIDE OF Wink's house was just as cluttered and chaotic as you'd expect a house to be with so many dogs and kids running wild. The kitchen was long and rectangular. I saw baskets of brown eggs on the wooden counter, and bowls of apples and bags of potatoes and onions. There were pots hanging from hooks on the ceiling, and a pile of folded laundry on the end of the table, and everything looked neat and tidy, in its own messy way.

The walls were a bright turquoise blue and there was a working woodstove in the corner. Everything smelled like gingerbread, and Wink's mother offered me a square piece as I waited. She was a short woman with big curves and wary green eyes and long red hair, no gray. She wore her hair in thick braids that crisscrossed her head in a style that looked both ancient and also sort of artsy and modern. She had on a black blouse-y shirt thing and a long skirt, lots of colors, and black boots with complicated laces. She looked like what you'd expect a fortune-teller to look like . . . but she also just looked like a mom. A mom who liked to dress interesting and cool instead of wearing beige pants and pastel-colored cardigans.

My own mother was a cool dresser. She was a writer and wanted people to know it. She had big round tortoiseshell glasses and thick brown hair and swooping, draping clothes that she wore with plain brown cowboy boots. People used to stare at her when she went grocery shopping, and she liked it that way. So Wink's mother made me feel right at home.

The cake was dark, almost black. It tasted like ginger and molasses. I ate it at the counter. Sticky little hands kept reaching up to the cake pan as I stood there, and it disappeared, piece by piece. The Orphans asked me questions as they took the gingerbread, fast, one after another, not waiting for my answers, like the questions were the only thing that mattered—

*What's your name?*

*Do you believe in ghosts?*

*Have you seen the ghost that lives in your house?*

*How fast can you run?*

*Have you ever played Follow the Screams?*

*Do you have any dogs?*

*Do you like sailboats?*

I tried to count the kids. I did. But they all kept moving around, and they all had red hair and green eyes, except for one dark-haired, brown-eyed girl who smiled at me sweetly as she took her second piece of gingerbread. I decided there were five of them, give or take. They ran circles around Wink's mother as she started making soup on the stove, and eventually ran out of the house, screen door slamming, followed by three smiling dogs, two big golden retrievers and one small white terrier.

And after my life so far, after all the quiet, especially now that Alabama and my mother were off in France . . . you'd think the pandemonium would have stressed me out. But no. I liked it.

I heard footsteps on the stairs, and Wink returned, wearing a green dress that seemed kind of old-fashioned. But what did I know about clothes. I usually just wore black pants and black button-downs, like Alabama. He liked to dress like Johnny Cash, or a gunslinger, minus the guns, and I figured if it was good enough for Alabama, it was good enough for me.

Wink's red hair was still crazy and wild. It bounced out around her little heart-shaped face and made her look even smaller and younger. She smiled at me, and I smiled back.

"How was the gingerbread?" she asked.

"Great."

"You met the Orphans."

"Yes."

"Can Mim read your cards?"

To my credit, I just nodded.

Wink's mother spun around from the stove and ushered me into the closest chair at the long wooden kitchen table. She pulled a stack of worn tarot cards from some hidden pocket near her hipbone and held them out to me.

"Pick three."

I did, and set them on the table. Wink and her mother leaned over me.

Wink pointed to the first card. "The Three of Swords."

"The Three of Swords is the card of loss, and broken relationships," Mrs. Bell said. Her voice wasn't dreamy or mystical, it was practical and matter-of-fact, like she was talking about the weather. "Things that are missing will not be found again. The Two of Swords is the card of tough choices, but the Three of Swords . . . you've already come to terms, and made your decision. Your feet are set on a path. Whether the path will be the right one . . ." She shrugged.

Wink pointed to the next two cards.

A naked man and woman looking up at an angel.

A crowned king in a chariot, two horses in front.

"The Chariot and the Lovers." Wink smiled.

"What do they mean?" I asked. But Wink just shrugged and kept smiling a mysterious Mona Lisa smile.

My mother had written a mystery a few years ago called *Murder by Tarot*. She visited several tarot readers in Seattle for research. She later told me and Alabama that some of the readers had been charlatans, some had been keen observers of human nature, and some had been inexplicably and eerily accurate. And as far as she could tell, the true readers had no connecting factors. Some were old, some young, some were bright-eyed and animated, some were quiet and detached. One of them had even guessed my mother's deepest secret . . . a secret she'd never told anyone. When Alabama and I asked her what the secret was, she just turned away and didn't answer.

Mrs. Bell, job done, lost interest in me and went back to

the stove. Wink stood by my chair, not saying anything.

I got up and took her hand. We walked through the kitchen, out the screen door, slam, across the yard, dogs barking happily, and headed into the deep dark woods, toward the setting sun.

A MILE OF pine needles crunching underfoot, darkness descending, trees tall and black, twisting forest path, cool night air. It got cold at night up in the mountains. Even in summer.

Wink was holding my hand and not saying a word.

Poppy had said I should get to know Wink. That we should be friends. But I wasn't just obeying her orders. There was really nowhere I wanted to be more than walking side by side, step by step, with this Bell girl.

Her fingers moved in mine. Tightened.

"Wink?"

She looked at me.

"What's it like? What's it like growing up on a farm with a bunch of brothers and sisters and a mom that reads tarot cards?"

She shrugged. "Normal." She paused for a second. "Isn't your mom an author? What's it like to have a mother who makes up stories for a living?"

I shrugged back at her. "Normal."

I didn't go into it all, about Mom leaving with Alabama. I just didn't feel like making myself sad. And Wink was bound to guess anyway, when she didn't see my mom or brother around all summer.

The creepy mansard-roofed Roman Luck house came into view, four tall chimneys pressing at the dark sky. I stopped and caught my breath.

Maybe it was because we were in the middle of the woods, near an abandoned house, trees on all sides and no-one-to-hear-you-scream, but I got a bad feeling all of a sudden.

Everything was dark. Thick, thick silence.

And then I heard a laugh.

And another.

Muffled voices.

More laughter.

And then came the flames. Orange and silky, waving at the sky.

A kid stepped back from the pile of wood, smiling, the way boys do whenever they manage to start a fire.

I looked around.

Damn it.

We'd walked right into the middle of a Poppy party.

Poppy's parties were quiet, secret things, made up of the Yellow Peril and a few sycophants. The parties moved around. Sometimes they were in Green William Cemetery, or on the overgrown main street of one of the nearby abandoned gold rush towns, or by the Blue Twist River.

Sometimes I was invited to her parties. Mostly not.

The Yellow Peril were Poppy's inner circle—it was a reference to opium, because, you know, Poppy. But everyone just called them the Yellows. Two guys and two girls and none of them half as evil or as beautiful as her. Poppy liked to lead the guys on and would give all her attention to Thomas one week and then Briggs the next. Just to keep them on their toes. The girls were Buttercup and Zoe. They dressed like twins, though they weren't. Always in black dresses, red lipstick, striped socks, and a twin set of cunning looks in their eyes. But Buttercup was tall and had black hair to her waist and Zoe was tiny and had short brown curly hair and both were pretty but definitely not sisters. I'd never spoken directly to them in my whole life. They didn't matter. Not when there was Poppy.

Poppy.

The Yellows surrounded her like rays around the sun. She wore knee-high boots and a short, swinging yellow skirt that barely covered the parts it needed to cover. She had a blue silk scarf around her slender neck, and her thighs were long and so damn creamy it made me feel sick.

God, I hated her.

I longed to grab Wink and run back the way we'd come.

I shook it off, and kept walking.

The Yellows all looked at me in that pitying way, like usual, but I just gave Poppy a cool nod and marched right on by, Wink at my side, like we were welcome. Like we'd been invited.

The bonfire was now six-foot flames clawing up, almost reaching the sagging roof of the Roman Luck porch, but not quite. We went up to it and the heat hit my skin in a rush. It felt good. I looked down at Wink, and she had her eyes closed, facing the warmth.

I didn't look back at Poppy and the Yellows.

I saw five or six non-Yellow kids from school. Perfect clothes and perfect shiny hair. The only time the Yellow-wannabes had ever noticed me was when Alabama was around. Then the girls would talk to me in a really sweet voice, to show Alabama how nice they could be to his unpopular brother.

Everyone was whispering instead of yelling and laughing, and there was no music playing—the Yellows wouldn't stand for it. Poppy liked quiet at all her parties.

A girl named Tonisha was handing out mason jars of frothy, amber-hued beer from a nearby keg. I knew it was probably a micro-brewed IPA, because the Yellows didn't drink anything cheap, but I declined to take one, and so did Wink. A wind came up out of nowhere and leaves rustled on the trees, whoosh, all at once, in that way that always gives me goose bumps.

Wink's fingers tightened again. I looked down at her.

The contrast with Poppy was profound.

Straight, blond, shining hair.

Red, frizzy, curly hair.

Tall, thin.

Short, small.

I knew one's body, every dip, every inch, every toe, every bend.

The other had her hand in mine and it was the first time we'd ever touched.

Both were a mystery.

"Wink?"

She glanced up at me.

"I think I'm going to like having you Bells as my new neighbors."

She nodded, face very serious. "We'll be good for you."

I smiled at that.

"Your brothers and sisters ask a lot of questions."

She nodded again. "They do that to people they like."

We were speaking in short snappy statements, and it was nothing like before, on the steps of my house, when Wink was either sweetly talking on and on about *The Thing in the Deep* or being calmly silent, the breeze in her hair. I supposed she was hating it here, at Poppy's party. I sure as hell was. What was so fun anyway about standing in the dark, whispering and drinking beer?

Maybe I'd made a mistake, not turning and running back down the path. But damn it, I didn't want Wink to think I was a coward. I'd been a coward long enough.

"This is a bad house," Wink said suddenly, looking up, way up, at the sagging roof. "The Roman Luck house is *not* lucky. It never was."

The Roman Luck house was a mile from town, and a mile from the Bell farm, right in the middle. It had sat empty for years, and houses went downhill fast when no one was taking care of them. All the bushes were overgrown, the front lawn covered with pinecones. The gravel road that led to the house from town was nothing but a stretch of brown pine needles and saplings, struggling to grow in the gloom.

I joined Wink in staring up at the house. Big and gray and going to ruin. The bay windows were broken, and I could see the shadow of the decaying grand piano that I knew was inside. We'd all explored the Luck house when we were younger. Dared each other to go in, to put our fingers on the chipped ivory keys, to climb up the wobbly, creaking stairs, to lie down on the dusty, rat-chewed quilt that still covered the master bed.

I'd been surprised that Poppy wanted to have her party here. Fearless Poppy, who wasn't afraid of anything . . . except this, the Roman Luck house. Not even the Yellows knew how much she hated the place. Just me. I'd been with her last summer, right beside her as she'd climbed the porch steps and then refused to go past the doorway, like a dog catching a bad scent. She laughed and said haunted houses were stupid. But her perfectly painted toes in their delicate, expensive sandals never crossed the rotting threshold.

Roman Luck's disappearance was our town's greatest mystery. He'd been young, and single, a doctor at the hospital where Poppy's parents worked now. And when he bought a grand house outside of town, in the middle of the woods, and filled it with grand things, people thought he was going to marry some pretty girl and live happily ever after. But he never did. He lived in the house for two years, and he never threw a party, or invited people over for supper. And then, one morning, he didn't show up for work. Days went by. When the police finally broke down the front door they found the inside frozen in time, as if Roman had just stepped outside for a breath of fresh air. There was a coffeepot on the table, stone cold, and a plate with a moldy, half-eaten sandwich. The milk had curdled in the fridge. The radio was even still on, playing sad old Delta blues songs . . . or so went the rumors.

"If I told you what happened to Roman, you wouldn't believe me," Wink said out of nowhere, like she could read my mind. Her shoulders shrugged up and disappeared into her messy red hair.

I took the bait. "Yes I would, Wink. I'd believe you."

Wink shook her head, but she was smiling.

"Let me guess. Ghosts drove Roman Luck screaming into the night, and now he's off in an asylum somewhere, stark raving mad."

She shook her head again. "The house is haunted, but that's not why Roman left. Sometimes people just leave, Midnight. They realize they are on the wrong path, or that they are in the wrong story, and they just go off in the middle of the night and leave."

Here was my chance. Here was the opportunity for me to say that I knew all about people leaving, that my mom took my brother and left, not in the middle of the night, but she left all the same.

The moment was slipping by, slipping, and I was letting it . . .

Wink gave me a searching kind of look, like she knew what I was thinking anyway. "Mim once read cards for a very, very old woman who used to live in Paris. She told my mother that she had an apartment there, on the Right Bank, still filled with her furniture and dresses and everything. She hadn't been back since World War II. She said that one day she decided she was done with Paris, and the war, and she never went there again."

"Is that true, Wink?"

"Of course it's true. All the strangest stories are true."

And then we both abruptly stopped talking. We just stood next to each other and didn't talk.

It was coming back, the feeling from earlier, the calm, peaceful feeling . . .

Laughter.

I looked up.

The Yellows were staring at us. Poppy too. She said something and they laughed again. And then she repeated it. Louder.

"I bet Feral Bell has little-girl underwear on. I bet she still wears white cotton panties with polka dots or butterflies. What do you say, Yellows? Should we find out?"

"Shut up, Poppy." And I tried to say it cool, say it how Alabama would say it, but I must have done it wrong, because Poppy just smirked at me, long and slow.

I looked at Wink and her face was serene. Calm.

"Grab them," Poppy said.

And the Yellows were on us. The guys held my arms and I couldn't move. Buttercup and Zoe went for Wink, and she didn't budge, didn't even flinch. Just stood there, looking peaceful. Almost like she'd been expecting this all along, and was glad to get it over with.

The non-Yellows gathered around. Watching. Waiting to

see what Poppy would do next. Tonisha and Guillermo and Finn and Della and Sung. Rich shiny hair. Rich shiny clothes. Rich shiny faces.

"Don't," I said. "Don't, Poppy. Please." I didn't even try to sound like my brother this time.

But her arms shot out and grabbed the edge of Wink's green dress, and yanked it up.

Wink's skinny white legs, red socks to her knobby knees.

Wink's underwear. White, with little unicorns on them.

Just as Poppy had predicted.

Poppy pointed. "See?" she said.

And laughed.

And laughed.

# POPPY

LEAF GRADUATED AND left. I was sixteen and I wasn't sure I had a heart, until it fucking broke in two, ripped shreds and veins and blood everywhere. He didn't even tell me where he went, just up and off and I even saw him the day after graduation, standing on the road at the end of my street, waiting for the bus, the sun setting behind him, green duffel bag over his shoulder. I would have thought he did it on purpose, caught the bus where I was bound to see him, except that would have meant Leaf thought about me, and I knew he didn't.

He gave me a nod as he climbed the steps, that's it, like I was a fucking postman or a stranger in the street. I tried to reach him, ran all the way, I was as good at running as I was at everything else. I tore, strained, but the doors shut, and the bus pulled away, and that was the last time I saw him.

I'd sworn that I'd never let a boy steal me, steal my heart, my mind, any single part of me. I'd sworn it over and over since I was old enough to know the difference.

But my knees hit the pavement with a crack anyway, and I lost it, I totally lost it, one second, two seconds, head hanging, eyes gushing, but people could see, they might be watching. I got back up, and left two bloody scrapes on the sidewalk where my kneecaps had been.

I thought about finding Zoe and Buttercup and spilling my guts and telling them my secrets. I could see them in my head, black dresses and striped socks, patting my shoulders and graciously tolerating my new vulnerability while losing respect for me with every tear that slid down my face.

I went over to the Hunt house instead and lost my virginity to Midnight.

# WINK

I BARELY EVEN noticed when the Wolf did what she did at the Roman Luck house. My head was all caught up in the unforgivables, who were bothering me, even with the sugar, so I'd started thinking up a plan to get rid of them for good.

I decided to show Midnight the hayloft. The hayloft is where events happen and plots unfold and I wanted events to happen and plots to unfold.

# MIDNIGHT

WINK DIDN'T CRY or anything. I don't know why I thought she would. The Bells never cried. That's one of the reasons they were impossible to bully.

She was quiet as I walked her back home, but then, she'd been pretty quiet the whole night. And I didn't know her well enough to know if that's how she usually was anyway. She didn't talk in school, but neither did I, and it didn't prove a thing.

"Do you want to see the hayloft, Midnight?"

We stepped out of the trees and back onto her farm. Two of the dogs got up from where they were sleeping in the long grass near the chicken coop. They shook themselves and came over to greet us, soft, warm tongues on my cold hands.

"Yes I do, Wink."

And she smiled, lips parting slightly, eyes bright. Just like that. Like she'd already forgotten that her dress had been pulled up and her unicorn underwear seen by a dozen kids from school.

How did she do it? How did she not care?

I was in awe of her, all of a sudden.

I used to be in awe of Poppy. All those years ago, laughing at her blood-dripping knees at the edge of my driveway, her bicycle in a heap beside her.

That's how I used to be.

Wink's farmhouse was dark and I figured it must be around eleven. The lights were still on in my house across the road, though, which was typical. Dad often read and worked until deep into the night. We were both night owls. Mom and Alabama were morning people.

I walked over to the ladder I'd seen Wink on earlier. I put my hand on a rung, and started climbing. I'd never been a guy for heights—that was my brother, who used to go cliff-jumping at the alpine lake near Kill Devil Peak. But I'd never seen the point of risking your life for one good fall.

Up and up. My hands were sweaty and my right palm slipped. I looked down at Wink's red head, coming up beneath me, and felt all right again. I got to the top of the ladder and put one knee in the square opening, and then the other, and I was inside the hayloft.

Watery white moonlight streamed between the cracks in the boards, so I could see pretty well. Wink crawled in behind me, quick and easy like she'd done it a million times, which I guess she had.

The hay smelled nice. Kind of sweet and dry like sawdust. There were square bales of it everywhere, all over the big, airy, angled-ceiling room. Most were piled up against one wall, but the floor was covered in a thick carpet of hay too.

Wink picked up something from the ground, and then reached into her pocket with her free hand. I heard a *fzzt* sound, and then a flame cut through the darkness. She lit the lantern she was holding, and set it back down. The hayloft filled with shadows.

"Isn't that dangerous?" I asked. "A lantern with all this hay?"

Wink fluttered the fingers of both hands in a sweet-ish dismissive gesture. "We haven't set fire to anything yet."

I thought about Mrs. Bell, and how she let all her kids do whatever they wanted, and how they all were still alive and thriving, somehow. My own father was gentle and compassionate but his List of Forbiddens had been a mile long when Alabama and I were kids. He took full responsibility for our staying alive and we hadn't been allowed to go ice-skating on Troll Lake, or sledding down Alabaster Hill, or hike any lonely forest trails that might be hiding cougars or bears. It bothered Alabama more than me, since he was born with a death wish.

Sometimes I wondered if that's why my mother preferred Alabama, because he took risks and liked to put himself in danger and was cool and didn't care about things that didn't matter. Alabama had his dad's silk-black hair and high cheek-bones and narrow black eyes. And even though neither of us had ever met him, I had a feeling that Alabama's father was cool, and full of death wishes, just like my brother.

I suppose that's why my mother fell in love with him.

"It's for the horses," Wink said. She sank down on top of a two-foot pile of the thin blond sticks, heaved a great sigh, and looked . . . happy. "The hay, I mean."

"You have horses?" I saw a small, beaten-up table with two short stools at one end of the barn. There were toys every-where, balls and dolls and jump ropes and a scattered pack of playing cards and books and an old wooden rocking horse missing his tail.

Wink nodded and tucked her arms behind her head. "They live in a large fenced-in area near the old Gold Apple

Mine. Mim bought them off a man in Sleepy Peak—he said they were too old to ride. So now we just let them run wild back there in the summer. Some of the mine's buildings are still standing, and there's a little creek, but there's no road to it and no one ever goes back there. The horses have the run of the place. We round them up and keep them warm in here in the winter. Mim's got a soft heart for animals."

I sat down beside her and leaned back, just like she did, putting my arms behind my head. I thought the hay would be itchy, but it wasn't. "Why do you call your mother Mim?" I asked, since I was really starting to wonder.

Wink turned her head until her cheek rested on her upper arm. Her red eyebrows tilted toward each other. "Why, what do you call yours?"

Her face was two feet from mine but her hair was so big it spread out between us and tickled my chin. "I don't call her anything right now. She took my older brother, Alabama, and went to France a few months ago. She's a mystery writer and is setting a series there, something historical about the Cathars."

I let out a sigh of relief. That hadn't been as hard as I'd thought it would be.

Wink was the first person I'd told.

"When is she coming back?"

I shrugged. Wink reached out and put her fingers on my

right wrist, on the tender inner side. She moved her fingertips back and forth, kind of gentle and soft, sort of like how she petted the dogs earlier, right between their ears. Her hand felt small and warm and really, really nice.

"Why were you named Wink?" I asked, out of the blue.

She looked at me in that sweet, staring way she had. "I don't know. Why were you named Midnight?"

"My mom said it's because I was born at midnight, right at the stroke of twelve. But my dad says I was born near dawn, just as the sun was coming up. So who knows."

Wink just nodded, and went back to brushing her fingers across my wrist.

She was doing that thing again, that no-talking thing that made me feel dreamy and peaceful.

"I'm sorry," I said, after a while. "I'm so sorry, Wink. Poppy's got you on her radar now and it's my fault."

"It's all right," Wink said, whispery voiced. "She was just trying to embarrass you through me. She wanted to make you feel helpless."

Wink. For a girl with a lost-in-an-enchanted-forest look in her eyes, she didn't seem to miss much.

"Don't let her win, Midnight. Don't feel embarrassed or helpless. Then she'll have no power over you."

"Easier said than done." Wink had a heart-shaped freckle, right above the inner elbow hollow of her left arm. It matched her heart-shaped face. I wanted to touch it. I wanted to put the fleshy part of my thumb right on it.

She smiled at me, big, and it made her ears stick out until they looked elvish.

"So everyone saw my unicorn underwear, Midnight. So what. Repeat after me. *So everyone saw Wink's unicorn underwear. Who cares.*"

I grinned, and did it. *"So everyone saw Wink's unicorn underwear. Who cares."*

"There," she said, and laughed, and her laugh was full and high and chinkled like the keys on the toy piano I'd had as a kid. "In a hundred years, who will care about my unicorn underwear? Who cares right now? There are bigger things to think about."

"Bigger things like what?"

"Battles and wars. Lost causes and lost loves. Unsolved mysteries and magical rings and Here Be Dragons. Fairy paths. Child-eating witches and child-saving witches. Tinderboxes and saucer-eyed dogs."

It was the longest she'd talked so far and her voice got quieter and quieter toward the end until her words were almost a lullaby.

"I'm using my Putting the Orphans to Sleep voice," Wink said.

"I could go to sleep right here in the hay," I said. And yawned.

"Midnight?"

"Yeah?"

"What do you want to be?"

"You mean, what do I want to do, like whether I want to be a writer like my mom, or a rare book dealer like my dad?"

"Yes."

A breeze blew through the opening to the hayloft and rattled the lantern. The flame flickered and the shadows in the barn jumped.

"I want to be a treasure hunter."

I probably should have said something realistic and normal. Something like "professional soccer player" or "film director" or "private investigator."

I waited for her to laugh. Poppy would have laughed. But Wink just looked at me.

"I don't want to find relics, though, like the Arc of the Covenant. I want to find music, and art. I want to find lost Bach compositions in German monasteries. I want to track down the missing paintings of Vermeer and Rembrandt, and the lost plays of Shakespeare. I want to crawl through castles and dig through attics and search through cellars."

"You would be good at that," Wink said.

And I wasn't ashamed of my confession anymore, not a bit, even though I've never admitted my treasure-hunting dreams to anyone except Alabama.

Wink smiled at me, and her ears popped out again.

"What do *you* want to be?"

She made a soft *hmmm* sound. "I want to be a Sandman. I want to crawl in children's windows and blow softly on their necks and sprinkle sand in their eyes. I want to make up stories and whisper them in the children's ears and give them good dreams." She breathed in, and out, her skinny ribs rising in her strange green dress. "Sometimes I do this for the Orphans. When there's a thunderstorm and they're tossing and turning. I sit beside them and whisper until they sleep deep and quiet."

She was looking at the hayloft ceiling and I was looking at her. "What kind of stories do you make up?"

"Well, I have a story about a cruel, selfish witch girl named Fell Rose. She casts a spell on an entire village, and makes them all her slaves, makes them dance to her wishes like puppets on strings . . . all except a dark-haired boy named Isaac who figures out her weakness and takes away her powers."

"What happens?" I asked, all caught up already. "What happens to Fell Rose and Isaac?"

She turned her head to the side, and met my eyes. "They become friends." She paused. "The Orphans always fall asleep before I get to the end. But I think they become friends."

We both stopped talking for a while, and I soaked up the comfortable silence.

"How many brothers and sisters do you have?" I asked a little while later.

Wink didn't answer me, just made a *hmmm* sound again.

"What happened to your dad? Do you read tarot cards like your mother? Did your older brother Leaf really run off to the Amazon?"

I was spewing questions suddenly, but didn't feel embarrassed, not at all.

Wink just laughed, chinkle, chinkle. She stared at the high barn ceiling, stretched her arms above her head, and sighed. "There are five Orphans," she said, "not counting the one that left."

I found out later that there was pretty much no way of getting the direct truth out of Wink when she didn't want to give it. So that was all I got in response.

A few minutes went by and I watched Wink's profile in the shadowy barn light, her small doll nose and her pointed chin.

That morning I'd been standing next to my new home and looking at the farmhouse across the road and wondering if I'd finally managed to leave Poppy behind.

And now here I was, in a hayloft with Wink Bell, and more content than I'd been since Mom and Alabama and France.

"Are you going to get revenge?" Wink asked in her sleepy voice, out of the blue. "You picked the Three of Swords and I think it means that you plan to get revenge. I think you want to punish Poppy, like Thief punished The Thing in the Deep when he lured her out of the castle and into the open, so he could fight her under the blue sky, in the sun."

"Revenge on Poppy? No. All I want to do is get away from her."

"But heroes get revenge. That's what they do."

"I thought heroes saved people and brought about happy endings."

"Yes, but first comes the revenge and the making-wrong-things-right."

And I thought Wink was going to whisper something in my ear when she leaned in then, something else about heroes and thieves and vengeance and Fell Rose and the boy . . .

. . . so when she put her lips on mine, I jerked.

She held still for a second, and then tried again.

If I'd thought about it, I would have guessed that Wink would kiss like a little girl, since she still kind of looked like one. Sweet and tender and shy. Two quick pecks and then running away.

But her kisses were . . . hunger, and experience, and skill, and *want*.

She grabbed my arms and then my hair and brought my face down to hers and when my lips touched her neck, her skin was sweet as sugar.

# PoPPy

I HAD ACQUIRED the Yellows my sophomore year because people of my caliber need an entourage.

Thomas was so wounded and sad all the time, broken home and a dead baby sister and he was one of those people who felt things deeply, deeply, and Briggs was the opposite, feisty and temperamental and jaunty like the ankle-biting Pomeranians that live across the street. I drove Thomas and Briggs batshit crazy all year and they were just the icing on the cake, after Midnight.

I was the center, the sun, and they were all spinning around me . . .

*No Poppy, you're nothing. You're nothing at all.*

Leaf's voice in the back of my head, back of my heart, creeping up on me like a wolf in the woods. I liked to brag to him that I wasn't scared of anything, but he knew. He knew that deep down I'm terrified I'll get old and ugly and it will all catch up to me, and my cruelty will echo through my wrinkles and liver spots and everyone will stop doing what I want or listening to me or even worse, forget about me altogether.

But I plan on dying when I'm still young and beautiful like Marilyn Monroe, just watch me.

Buttercup was the daughter of a martial arts movie star who was never around. He left her here in Broken Bridge along with his wife, and only came back for holidays, and Buttercup's mother was tall and beautiful and elegant, long swinging black hair, like mother, like daughter. I'd seen her once at the farmers' market and once in the bookstore, but I don't think she spoke English, not very well.

Zoe was the leader of the two, even though Buttercup did all the talking. Zoe liked to stand in her shadow publicly, but secretly she made all the decisions, called all the shots, people can surprise you that way, if you pay attention, which mostly I don't. Zoe came from a loving family, her parents were loaded and liberal, and let her do and be whatever she wanted, as in, if she turned to them one day and said, *Mom, Dad, I've decided that I want to be a banana, that's who I am,* they'd be like, *We'll pick up some yellow fabric in town.*

I half hated Zoe most the time for this, but sometimes I was just kind of enraptured with her too, like how people fawn over the UK royals, scrambling after each tiny golden tidbit of glittering personal info like starving dogs. I basked in her sunshiny life and daydreamed about being a tiny pixie girl with brown curls and parents that didn't give a damn in all the right ways.

Once upon a time Zoe and Buttercup and I were rubbing gravestones in the Green William Cemetery because that's what they wanted to do and I was trying to be more charitable and let them get their way sometimes. The weather had turned and the sun was gone and Leaf found me as I was scraping my charcoal piece over my thousandth *Here lies the body of,* the dark clouds bounding in.

He told me to follow him and I did, dropping the tracing paper and the charcoal without another word to Zoe and Buttercup, I didn't even think of them, they didn't even exist anymore. We went to the woods and I told Leaf how I was trying to be better, how I wasn't so bad, not really, not in my inner deeps, I was only bad when I *wanted* to be at least, I could help it, I could stop anytime. He laughed and said I was hopeless and sad. But when I pressed myself into his bony ribs he pressed back. He put his palms on my cheeks and his lips on my forehead and he just held me *and held me and held me* until the sky cracked and the rain started pouring.

I swore to be better then, to give it all I had, to put my whole heart in it until I felt it straining. I'd be nicer to my parents, try to be what they thought I was, I'd be a better friend to Zoe and Buttercup, I'd stop torturing all the boys and let them move on and find someone who could love them back. I could do it, I really could, keep it up, Poppy, keep it up, keep it up.

It would last a few hours, all the good intents, a few days even, but then I'd snap back, cruel, cruel, cruel, relishing every little lick of it on my tongue.

I SHOULDN'T HAVE kissed the Hero. The kissing was supposed to come at the very end. After the monster, and the fight. After the glass coffin and the pinprick of blood. But Midnight was lying there in the hay and his eyes were sad, and his hair was curling on the apple of his cheek. I wanted to hold his heart in my hand, reach into his chest and cradle it in my palm, like one of Nah-Nah's newborn kittens with its frail tiger stripes and its eyes still closed.

I read the Orphans a fairy tale once called Giant, Heart, Egg. It was about a troll who kept his heart hidden in an egg in a distant lake, so he couldn't be killed. I wished Midnight's heart was hidden far away in a distant lake. I wanted to stand guard over it. I wanted to cast magic spells and train dragons to protect it. I wanted to make sure it would be safe until happily ever after.

Leaf said that reading a book out of order was dangerous, because things were supposed to happen one, two, three, four, five. And if they didn't, if four went before two, the whole world spun upside down and bad things came in the night.

What would happen now that I had put the end of my story in the beginning? Would my world spin upside down? Would Midnight's?

Leaf never talked. Almost never. He was like Pa. He was like the great horned owl with bloody talons in *The Witch Girl and the Wolf Boy*. He rarely spoke, and when he did, you listened.

Leaf once told me that there was absolutely no difference between the Orphans' fairy tales and the nose on my face, because both were only as real as I thought they were.

Sunlight on my cheeks.

The windows in my old bedroom, back at the house in town, faced west. So I woke to dim light even when the sky was blue.

But my creaky new bedroom was two big windows of full, dead east. I lifted my fingers and spread them out in the warm yellow sunshine, one behind the other, like I had superpowers. Like I was shooting sunlight laser beams.

My old bedroom had muted green carpet and white walls and a sensible closet.

My new bedroom had a warped old wardrobe that came with the house, a working fireplace, and a slanting hardwood floor that made a nice slapping sound when my feet hit it.

I'd taken down the dusty yellow curtains the day before and left the windows bare. So my room was just the bed, the bare windows, two black bookcases (full), and one dresser. Plus the aforementioned wardrobe. Nothing on the walls. I thought I might put up the map of Middle-earth that Alabama got me for Christmas, right over the bed, maybe. But nothing else. I liked the open space.

Mom used to say I was a minimalist. But Alabama was a pack rat like her, and their endless boxes of pack-rat things were now sitting in the musty brick basement, filling it to the brim. I wondered if they would ever come back for them, or just start acquiring new pack-rat things in France.

Dad didn't seem to mind the boxes. He didn't mind much of anything, concerning Mom and Alabama.

Dad loved my half brother just as much as he loved me . . . and maybe this should have pissed me off, since Alabama got most of my mom's love, and half my dad's as well. But I was sort of awed by my dad's capacity for loving a son who wasn't his blood. I think Alabama was too. He and Mom were of the same mind about pretty much everything, but with Dad . . . he always gave in, even when he didn't agree.

I used to catch Alabama standing in the doorway of Dad's office, watching him as he huddled over his rare books. He would have this soft look in his eyes, this small smile on his face, and the whole scene was kind of beautiful.

I missed my brother.

I went to the windows and put my palms on the sill and breathed in the green-smelling summer air, grass and dew and pine. The leaves on the apple trees twinkled in the morning sun like stars.

The light hit my bare chest, and I leaned into it.

I liked being out in the country. It suited me better than town.

Three red-haired kids were running around the Bell farm. The dogs were barking happily at a brown-and-white goat, and one of the kids had climbed on the goat's back and was shouting, *Tally-ho billy, tally-ho* . . . but the goat was just ignoring everyone, standing still and eating some wildflowers growing near an old red water pump.

I didn't see Wink.

I closed my eyes. That girl made me feel like I was dreaming. Broad daylight dreaming.

She would make a good Sandman, I guess.

After the hayloft kissing, Wink had cuddled into me, trusting and easy, like she'd been doing it her whole life. Her skinny legs nestled between mine, her palms spread open over my chest.

Her face pressed into my neck so tight I could feel it when she blinked, soft lashes on my skin.

I'd only ever kissed Poppy, before the hayloft. Poppy did everything flawless, perfect. She knew right where to put her lips, and yours.

And yet, Poppy's kisses were flimsy and soft, like butterfly wings or fresh bread crumbs.

But Wink kissed . . . deep.

Deep as a dark, misty forest path.

One that led to blood, and love, and death, and monsters.

She kissed with *yearning*.

I'd felt that yearning before. I'd yearned at Poppy all year, so hard I thought I might burst into flames, spontaneous yearning combustion. But I'd never felt any yearning back.

I stretched into the fresh air bouncing through my window, and smiled.

Who knew there was so much going on inside a small, red-haired girl with strawberry-buttoned overalls.

Alabama dated a lot of girls. A *lot* of girls. Girls went to him like flies to honey, like kids to puddles, like cats to shafts of sun.

I once asked him if he liked any over the others. If any of them meant anything. We were walking home from a late-night horror movie. I remembered Alabama's boot heels click-clacking on the cobblestone street that led to our old house.

My brother stopped walking and looked at me. He always wore his hair long, past his shoulders. He sometimes tied it back with a thin strap of leather, but not that night. It was blowing free in the summer breeze, flickering black then blue then black again in the yellow streetlight.

"Midnight, do you know Talley Jasper?"

I did. Talley was a puzzle. She had waist-long brown hair and played the cello—she was always lugging that big instrument around. She sat by herself at lunch, reading a book while she ate an apple. She was always eating apples. Her parents owned some overpriced clothing company, but she never acted like the other rich kids, spoiled and aggressive and entitled and loud. She was nice to the unpopular kids, and prickly with the popular ones. She once smiled sweetly at me when I accidentally stepped on her foot in the cafeteria. She said, "It's okay, Midnight," and then walked away, and I remembered being really pleased that she knew my name.

"Talley has more going on inside her head than anyone I've ever met. And someday I'm going to find out what. Meanwhile I'm just biding my time."

We started walking again, turned down our block. We reached Poppy's big house, perfect grassy lawn, perfect white pillars, perfect gazebo off to the side. I slowed down. Alabama slowed too.

"How do you know that, about Talley? How can you tell?"

"I just have a feeling." Alabama smiled. "Plus there was the time I ran into her late one night near the Blue Twist River, where it curves at the edge of town. She was just standing at the edge, watching the stars. She turned, caught me watching her, and then . . ." Alabama's eyes flashed the same way our mom's did when she was talking about a new idea for a book. "And then she grabbed me with both hands, clenched my shirt in her fists, reached up, and kissed me. And she never said a word. Still hasn't said a word to me. I once passed her in the hall at school, and I brushed her arm as I walked by. She looked up at me, and smiled, but kept on walking. That's it. So I wait."

Alabama chuckled, cool and lazy, and then mom called down from the upstairs window, wanting him to come help her with a bit in her story. He opened the door and went to her.

I was still full of Poppy-love when Alabama told me about Talley. It was last summer and I was caught up in her like a soft, white cloud in a black thunderstorm. I'd no idea what my brother was talking about.

Now I knew, though.

I wondered if Alabama missed Talley, in France. I wondered how long he was going to wait for her.

I FOUND MY dad in the attic. He'd taken it as his new office/ library, which meant that he'd had to move six million heavy boxes of books up two creaking flights of stairs the day before.

Dad liked to collect things, like Mom and Alabama did, but collecting was his business, so he had the excuse.

I gave him a mug of green tea. Mom and Alabama drank coffee and nothing else. And my dad drank green tea, and nothing else. I wasn't sure what I drank yet.

Dad took the tea, and sipped, and smiled. He was unloading old wrinkled-looking books and auction catalogs. Everything was a mess, which drove me kind of crazy. I liked things clean.

The angled ceiling meant my dad had to duck whenever he walked to the corners of the narrow, rectangular room. Exposed beams and dust. But he seemed to like it.

I noticed that he'd put up his wedding picture on his antique desk. My dad wasn't giving anything away about his true feelings regarding my mom leaving with my brother. So I looked for hints where I could.

I put my palms on the polished wood and leaned in closer.

My dad in a brown suit, looking big-eyed, deer-in-headlights. But my mom was wearing her wide, beautiful smile, the one that made her eyes go soft and twinkly.

And if sometimes I thought her smile in that picture looked genuine, but a bit strained, well, I was probably just reading into it.

"So you were talking to the oldest Bell girl yesterday," Dad said, not looking at me, his eyes on the green leather book in his hands.

"Yeah."

"I like her," he added.

But what he meant was, *I like her better than Poppy.*

My dad knew what Poppy was the moment she first walked through our door. He would have put her on the List of Forbiddens if he could have. Eli Hunt respected maturity like he respected privacy. He let us, both me and Alabama, make our own rules after we turned sixteen. For better or worse, I was in charge of my own life now.

# Poppy

THERE WAS A big thunderstorm a few years ago, it knocked down trees and houses and flooded the Blue Twist River, and everyone was super into it, it was exciting, destruction is exciting, no matter what they say. I went down to the river just to watch it rising, and to see what had been picked up in its stormy path, patio furniture, toys, dead animals.

I found Leaf standing on the bank, leaning against a tree,

inches from the muddy swirling rapids, doing the same fucking thing.

"It's beautiful," he said, after we'd been there in the pelting rain for a while and had both just watched a red wooden door go floating past, and then a blue bike, and then a pair of black boots, tied together by the shoelaces, and then a little fox, on its back, its dead paws on its belly.

I went to the hayloft a lot after Leaf left on the bus. Sometimes the Bell brats were in there but when they weren't I climbed the ladder and sat in the sun, hay, quiet.

And now Midnight was living by them, right across the street. I suppose he thought he was moving up in the world, and getting away from me, yeah, as if it would be that easy, as if, as if, why is everyone around me so undeniably dumb? I want to like people, I do, actually, but they're all just so *dumb*.

I'd already felt Midnight edging away from me before he moved out to that dumpy farmhouse. And then I found him talking to Feral on the steps and he was just so *into* her, into the red hair and freckles and weirdness, I felt sick just thinking about it.

Well, if Midnight wanted to be with Wink and her fairy tales and her hayloft and unicorn underwear and overalls, then I'd show him who she was. I'd really, really show him.

# WINK

MIDNIGHT FOUND ME as I was coaxing little blue eggs out
from underneath one of the pretty white Silkies. I brought
him inside to the kitchen and made poached yellow-eyes on
toast for him and the Orphans. You need a big boiling pot to
make poached yellow-eyes, which I like because using a big
boiling pot makes me feel like I'm a witchie.

Mim was in her reading room, so I made coffee too. She didn't
like me to drink coffee. She said it would give me dark dreams. I
didn't give any of it to the Orphans, just me and Midnight, sip-
ping from the same blue cup, fresh cream and brown sugar.

The Hero stood closer to me, after the hayloft. And he
looked at me different too.

I told him the names of the Orphans, and we picked strawberries from the garden. I showed him how to squish his
bare toes in the black dirt. We ate the berries ripe and juicy
and hot from the sun, like Laura and Lizzie at the Goblin
Market, *For your sake I have braved the glen, and had to do
with goblin merchant men. Eat me, drink me, love me. Hero,
Wolf, make much of me. With clasping arms and cautioning
lips, with tingling cheeks and fingertips, cooing all together.*

# MIDNIGHT

THE DAY SO far:

Gathering eggs, breakfast, playing hide-and-seek, weeding the big square garden between the house and the barn, playing fetch with the dogs, Mim making Caprese salad for lunch with golden olive oil and fresh-picked basil and tomatoes, us all eating it standing at the kitchen table, me drawing up a treasure map for the Orphans, us all following it to the back pasture, digging holes with rusty shovels, looking for treasure.

When the sun got too hot I went home to get my tools. Coins, handkerchief, cards, steel rings. They were in a box in the basement. I'd kept them hidden since Poppy found them several months ago and teased me about it for weeks. I did my magic tricks for Wink and company in the hayloft and the kids sat still and wide-eyed and didn't even talk. Wink watched me closely and smiled her big, ear-sticking-out smile at the end.

After I put my magic stuff away, Wink pulled *The Thing in the Deep* out of the pocket of her overalls and started reading. She sat on an old quilt spread over a pile of hay, barefoot, overalls, the Orphans around her, and me. The sun was streaming in the hayloft opening, low and hazy. Which was the only way I could tell how late it was. Time seemed to have stopped entirely. I hadn't had a day go by so dreamily, so lazily, since I was a little kid. Since before I understood the concept of time.

The tips of Wink's fingers were still stained from the strawberries, tiny, pink-red little flicks as she turned the pages. Her lips were stained too. I watched them as they moved with the words, mouth as red as blood.

Bee Lee cuddled up next to me, head against my side.

The Orphans consisted of three boys and two girls. All redheads, except for Bee, who had deep brown hair. Bee had just turned seven years old. I knew this, because it was one of the first things she told me. The twins were Hops and Moon, the oldest boy was Felix, and last of all was tiny Peach, the youngest. The ten-year-old twins were the wildest. They always seemed to be trying to outdo the other. Who could scream the loudest? Who could get the dogs howling? Who could put the most hay down the other's shirt? After that came Peach, who was about five or six, but had the same loud, rascally fierceness of the twins. Felix was maybe fourteen and had the look of his older brother, Leaf, about him. He was quieter than the others, though his eyes were lively enough.

Bee Lee was already my favorite. She was cuddly and sweet like the Bichon Frisé I'd had when I was little. She was always trying to squeeze her hand into mine, or put her dimpled little arm around my waist.

Wink had a beautiful reading voice. Delicate and slow. She read about Thief, about the death of his father, and the prophecy. She read about his journey into the Cursed Woods, just him and the clothes on his back and the sword his father left him. She read about how he needed to steal food, apples from orchards and pies from windowsills, to keep himself from starving. She read about how he sat by his small fire at night and sang the old songs to keep his loneliness at bay.

We heard Mim call out *dinner* just as Wink read the last word of the fifth chapter. She slipped the book back in her pocket. The Orphans jumped up and took off for the house, Bee Lee giving me a shy smile over her shoulder before darting down the ladder.

I looked at Wink, and she was looking at me.

"Should we go to dinner?" I asked.

She shrugged.

I got to my knees. I put my fingers on the small of her back, and kissed her belly button, right through her cotton overalls. She put her hands on my head, her strawberry-stained fingertips in my hair. I turned my chin, and leaned my cheek against her.

*"What the hell is this?"*

I jerked. Wink's hands dropped to her sides. I opened my eyes. Closed them. Opened them again, let go of Wink, and stood up.

Poppy.

Wink stepped backward, a quiet sidle into the corner shadows. Poppy ignored her. She was wearing another short, swoopy sort of dress, the kind that showed more than it hid. It was green, the same color as Wink's eyes.

"You weren't home and your dad wouldn't tell me where you'd gone. He's always hated me." She paused, and ran her hand down her hair, smoothing it, drawing attention to it. "But I figured it out."

"You're trespassing," I said. "This is Wink's farm. You're not welcome. She doesn't want you here."

Poppy laughed.

She grabbed me by the front of my shirt and yanked me toward her. Then she narrowed her eyes at the darkness behind me. "Is that true, Feral? You don't want me here?"

Wink stayed in the shadows.

Poppy let go of my shirt and walked into the dark. She wrapped her fingers around the right strap of Wink's overalls and pulled her, one step, two, back into the fading evening light at the center of the hayloft. Wink followed, meek as a lamb.

Poppy brushed a curly strand of Wink's hair off her cheek. Wink didn't stop her.

"Do you think Midnight is a prince come to rescue you from being a loser?" Poppy kept her fingers on Wink's face. "Is that what you think? I bet you kissed him last night, after you showed everyone your unicorn underwear at the party. I bet you crawled all over him. You Bells—you're nothing but animals. Dirty and sex-crazed like a bunch of smelly goats."

*"Stop it, Poppy."*

I didn't scream it. I didn't even raise my voice. But she took her hand from Wink's cheek and turned around.

"You protecting your new little girlfriend, Midnight? Wow, that's adorable." She put her hand on her hip and twitched her torso until her dress swung against her upper thighs, swish, swish. "How can you stand it? How can you stand kissing such a pasty, freckled, dirty thing? Is it just hormones? Is this some kind of Testament to the Male Organ? Should I be taking notes? Putting together an academic study?"

"You're so *mean*." I said it quiet, really quiet, but she was listening. "Why are you always so mean? What's wrong with you? Were you born like this? Sometimes I think there must be a hole in your heart . . . one that hurts and makes you roar like an animal with its leg in a trap. Is that it, Poppy? Is that why?"

Poppy just stared at me. An evening breeze blew in and stirred the hay and we all just stood there.

She turned.

Walked to the ladder.

Climbed down.

Left.

And then Wink was at my side, slipping her hand into mine. "Let's go to dinner," she said.

And without even looking, I knew she was smiling. I could hear it in her voice, sense it in her fingers, strawberry tips pressing into my palm.


# POPPY

"YOU STARE AT Leaf Bell. You stare at him a lot."

"A lot," Zoe echoed, her stupid brown pixie curls twitching as she nodded her head, her and Buttercup both looking at me. The two of them lived next door to each other, had always lived next door to each other. They showed up in kindergarten doing the creepy, creepy twin thing, same clothes and repeating each other's sentences and talking in unison. They have different hair and different skin and different eyes, and one's tall and one's tiny, but for a long time I could barely tell them apart. Though to be honest I never really tried.

We were sitting in the bleachers, done running, wet hair from the showers making damp trails down our T-shirts. Buttercup and Zoe ran in black shorts and black shirts, and striped socks pulled up to their knees, it would have been less laughable if they didn't take it so seriously.

The boys were on the track, Leaf in front, he was always in front. He was the best runner at our 1,300-kid school, we took state the last two years and he was why.

"Leaf is vile." Buttercup.

"All the Bells are vile." Zoe.

"Aren't they?" They said that last bit together, twinsy style.

"Shut up, Buttercup. Shut up, Zoe."

And then they swapped a secret, knowing smile. I felt like slapping it off their faces but instead I told them that if they ever mentioned Leaf's name again I would spread a rumor that I'd caught the two of them kissing the hot new math teacher Mr. Dunn in the cemetery, back by the Redding mausoleum, long grass hiding them from view. Details make a lie, it's all in the details, Buttercup and Zoe knew this by now. I'd taught them.

And they never said his name again, even on the day he left, even after I told them about Midnight, and what I'd done.

When I found Midnight in the hayloft with his cheek against Wink's stomach and her hands in his hair . . . the expression on his face . . . and Feral looking down at him . . . There was something happening between them, something not in the plan.

Leaf gone.

And now Midnight.

Not again. Not again, not again, not again, not again.

## WINK

THE HERO DOES magic tricks. Not real ones, like Mim and Leaf, but the sweet kind that don't have any true magic in them at all. He showed them to me and the Orphans in the hayloft.

Bee Lee stared at him all through dinner. Bee's got a soft heart, like the red-eyed Banshee in *Piety Shee and the Moonlight Dancers*. Piety wandered the earth looking for a lost love, her nighttime wails like willows sighing in the wind.

Bee Lee's been missing Leaf since he left, and Felix doesn't pay attention to her in the same way—they're too close to the same age, Mim says. But Midnight . . . she looked at him all dazzly-eyed and he didn't mind a bit.

The Wolf came to the hayloft again, but Midnight did what

he was supposed to do. He defended me, like a Hero. He drove her away, back into the darkness.

Mim read my tea leaves again, later, after Midnight went home. But she wouldn't tell me what they said.

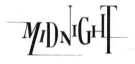

## MIDNIGHT

THE YELLOWS WERE standing in a semi-circle, eating plump red cherry tomatoes out of a brown paper bag.

Wink and I had gone into town to visit the Carnegie, and our backpacks were heavy with books. We ate olive oil ice cream from the little Salt & Straw stand on one corner, and got Parmesan and butter popcorn from Johnny's popcorn Shack on the other. Dusk was coming on, and the shadows were growing long. The air smelled like wildflowers, and grass, and snow. In the mountains the air always smells like snow. Even in summer.

We walked down the click-clacking cobblestones of Dickenson Rose Lane, waved to my old house, ignored Poppy's, petted a chill St. Bernard through a white fence, and then went through the Green William Cemetery, toward the woods.

The Yellows were blocking the Roman Luck path. The

Roman Luck path was the shortcut that led to the Roman Luck house, and the Bell farm, and it was our only way home, unless we wanted to walk three extra miles out on the regular roads. And it was almost dark.

Buttercup and Zoe popped tomatoes into each other's mouths, bright red lips closing around bright red tomatoes. Their black dresses and striped socks jarred with the lush trees behind them. They both had on matching skull-shaped backpacks, though school was long out. Buttercup's black hair was in a tight, sleek braid and Zoe had slicked down her short curls and looked like a thirties movie star. They gave us the side-eye while they chewed, tomato seeds on their chins.

Thomas and Briggs were standing with arms crossed and heads leaning away from each other. Deliberately. They must be fighting over Poppy. Again.

Buttercup and Zoe both swallowed, and then spoke at the same time. "Hello, Midnight. Hello, Feral."

They'd never talked directly to me before. I'd never mattered enough.

Where was Poppy? She put them up to this, no doubt, so where the hell was she?

"If you want to use the path you have to pass a test," Buttercup said, and nodded her oval face, quick, quick, black braid swishing.

"You have to pass a test," Zoe repeated.

Thomas and Briggs just stared at us, and ate more tomatoes. Thomas was tanned and blond and attractive in that wounded, sad way that girls always liked. And Briggs was lanky and witty and good at sports and rich as hell. They could have had any girl, but they were Poppy's pawns, just like I used to be.

I sighed. "What are you talking about, Buttercup?"

"It's a kissing test. You have to pass a kissing test." Nod, nod.

"What's a kissing test?" Wink asked, voice low, hands in deep pockets.

"You both have to kiss each other, and then you both have to kiss Poppy, and then we vote. If we like what we see, we let you enter the forest." Zoe this time. She took Buttercup's hand, fingers intertwining. They both turned to us, twin wicked smiles.

Briggs threw a tomato up in the air and caught it in his mouth, perfect and fluid, like he was posing for an All-American Boy poster. "I don't know why we didn't think of this before," he said, still chewing. "It's brilliant. Tomorrow I'm going to stand on Blue Twist Bridge and make people kiss before they can pass. And maybe charge them money too."

"Like the Three Billy Goats Gruff," Wink said. Softly.

"What do you mean?" Briggs's eyes snapped on hers. "Are you calling me a billy goat?"

Wink just shrugged and looked tranquil.

"I'm not a goat, Feral Bell. *You're* the goat. That's right, Poppy told us about how you and Midnight were up in the hayloft, doing beastly things—"

"It's a fairy tale." Thomas stepped closer to Wink, almost protectively. And it kind of pissed me off, because wasn't that my job? But I understood it too, because Wink had that effect on a guy.

"What the fuck are you talking about?" Briggs cocked his head and flared his nostrils.

"The Three Billy Goats Gruff is a fairy tale about a troll that lives under a bridge and tries to eat anyone that passes. Everyone knows that story, Briggs."

Buttercup and Zoe nodded, very wisely. "Everyone," they said together. "Everyone knows it."

"Who the hell reads fairy tales? Fairy tales are for babies—"

Poppy stepped out from behind a tree. Gray dress matching her gray eyes, black boots to her knees. She smiled the same Cheshire Cat grin as Buttercup and Zoe, but she had her hands up in a submissive gesture.

"Peace, everyone. Peace. The next thing we know, we'll all be so distracted fighting that we won't notice when these two sneak off right underneath our noses, like they're the cunning, tricksy heroes and we're the simpleminded villains in a children's book."

She looked at me. *Glared* at me.

"And I'm not going to let that happen, because I want to see how your little unicorn underwear girlfriend kisses, Midnight. I want to make sure she's good enough for you. The Yellows are going to watch us all and then help me decide if I can allow a past lover of mine to be with this freckled little barnyard girl."

My mind started racing with all the fighting things Alabama had told me: *Stay relaxed, bend your knees, kicking isn't sissy, be prepared to run . . .*

"Five against two, I don't care. We're not doing it, Poppy. I'd let your Yellows beat me bloody before I'd make Wink kiss you."

But suddenly Wink's hand was on my arm, and she was moving it back and forth in that gentle way she had. "It's all right, Midnight. Let's just do it and move on." She got on her tiptoes, lips to my ear. "They want you to fight them. Don't give them what they want. Let's just play along and act like we don't care."

She put her heels back on the ground, turned, and walked up to Poppy. She placed her freckled hands on Poppy's flawless cheeks, ran her thumbs over Poppy's arched blond eyebrows, pulled her face down . . .

And kissed her.

No one had ever taken Poppy by surprise before. Not ever.

One second . . . two . . .

And then Poppy's shoulders relaxed, her eyes closed . . .

Her lips started moving under Wink's . . .

The kiss went on. And on. Soft and slow and lips and girl, girl, girl.

Thomas and Briggs stopped eating tomatoes and looking sulky and aggressive. They leaned forward, shoulders almost touching.

. . . the kiss . . .

Buttercup and Zoe held hands and stared. Zoe's mouth was open a little bit.

. . . the kiss . . .

The light was now an eerie twilight blue, and the forest had gone dark, and we'd promised Mim we'd be home an hour ago.

. . . the kiss . . .

Wink pulled back. Just like that. Snap. She put her hands back in her pockets, spun around, and came back to me.

"Your turn," Wink said, and gave me her ear-popping smile.

I didn't do it.

I just took Wink's hand and walked right past the stunned-looking Poppy and the stunned-looking Yellows, right into the dusky black woods, not another word.

No one tried to stop us. No one said anything at all, except Poppy, who called out my name, just once. But I didn't turn around.

# Poppy

THAT PERT PERT pert little redhead.

Things were starting to get a little out of control, but I knew I could handle it, I'm Poppy, for fuck's sake. I never give up, ever, I don't have it in me.

I told Briggs to meet me at midnight in my backyard between the lilac bushes and then I told Thomas to come to my bedroom at eleven and we were both mostly naked when Briggs found us, just as I'd planned, Thomas with his hands sliding up my bare back and me with my face in his blond hair and my knees gripping his hipbones, just as he liked.

Thomas's younger sister died, she drowned in the Blue Twist River when she was eight years old, and Thomas was supposed to be watching her when it happened. Their father went crazy, he's in an institution and is considered dangerous to himself and others, and Thomas, oh how sad he is, how he worries about me whenever I hang out at the river, worries

I'll slip in and disappear in an instant, just like his dead baby sister, and I like his sadness, I do, but it's not enough, not enough to stop me.

Briggs swore revenge on Thomas, like a character in a book, and I laughed out loud and asked if they were going to duel at sunrise because I'd like to place bets on who would kill who . . . and then Briggs turned his anger on me, and my *god* I had them both wrapped around my damn finger, it was *too* easy. Briggs said I was going to get what was coming to me, that I'd led them both on, and turned their friendship to ash, very dramatic, especially for Briggs, and it was all so perfect, I wouldn't have wished for more if I'd done it on a falling star.

Thomas started crying then, soft, quiet tears down his tanned cheeks, and I will say this, he was hot even when he cried, just like Midnight, and I felt a twinge in my heart then, just a twinge, just a flicker. Thomas didn't swear or make threats like Briggs, but then, the quiet ones are the ones you have to watch out for.

# WINK

THE HERO ATE dinner with us, and afterward he asked to see my bedroom, but I shared it with Peach and Bee Lee, so I didn't take him there. Mim had a late-night reading and the twins were camping in the woods. Felix had a girlfriend already, he was like Leaf in that way, and the two of them had claimed the hayloft. His girl was pretty and gentle, with rosy cheeks and bashful eyes, but Mim had given Felix the Bliss and Baby talk recently, so I wasn't worried.

The Three Billy Goats Gruff boy had dark hair and two different-colored eyes. Blue and green.

Different-colored eyes meant a lot of things.

A curse.

Bad luck.

Madness.

A withered soul.

A pact with the devil.

A family secret.

A lie.

A changeling.

A promise, un-kept.

I brought Midnight to the garden, and he stretched out down in the dirt with his head in the strawberries while I spelled out my secrets on his naked back, my fingers drawing the letters up his spine.

He asked me about my father again.

And Leaf.

He tried to get me to talk about my kiss with the Wolf.

But I wouldn't say a word.

## MIDNIGHT

"Midnight."

Warm breath on my skin. The covers rustled, a body next to mine, side to side, spoons. Was I dreaming? Was there a Sandman in my bed, whispering in my ear, blowing on my neck? I kept my eyes closed, stretched out my fingers. I wanted to tangle them in her tangled red hair.

But they slipped right through, water, silk.

I smelled jasmine.

Poppy.

"I climbed the drainpipe." She turned over, kissed my earlobe. Slow. "Two miles in the dark of night. I went through a forest and up a wall." She wriggled. Slithered. Soft skin everywhere. "Do I seem like the kind of person who would let a red-haired hayloft girl in unicorn underwear take what's mine? You are mine, Midnight. For as long as I want you."

Her lips on my neck, chest, stomach . . .

"Poppy, stop."

She didn't.

"Poppy, *stop.*"

She did.

"Fine. *Fine*, Midnight. Will you just put your arms around me, then? Can I get that much, at least?"

I did. I tucked her head under my chin and laid my hand flat across her lower belly, spreading out my fingers until they touched her hip.

She never let me hold her.

She was *that* worried about me and Wink, I guess.

She was right to be worried.

Just as I was falling back to sleep, eyelids closing, Poppy wriggled out of my arms and woke me up again. She went over to the window and looked out, over at the Bell farm, the moonlight settling around her. A breeze came in and moved the hair across the curve of her shoulder blades, back and forth, just an inch or two.

"You know, Leaf told me something about his crazy sister once." Poppy turned and grinned at me over her shoulder, the old foxy Poppy grin, the one from her gangly, knee-scraped days. "He said the Roman Luck house scared Wink out of her weird, addled little mind. He said it gave her nightmares as a kid, nightmares so bad she used to wet the bed."

Poppy laughed, quiet and hard and mean. "Maybe we should start calling her Tinkle. Tinkle Bell."

"Good one." I said it lazy and cool, like my brother, so she knew I didn't mean it.

"I think we should make Wink face her fear. What do you think, Midnight?"

Where was Poppy going with this? Wink hadn't seemed scared of the Roman Luck house when we were at the party. I'd have known, if she were scared. Wouldn't I?

Poppy snapped her fingers, one, two, three, and then glided back to the bed. She sat at the foot and crossed her naked legs, and looked so beautiful I wanted to throw myself out the window.

"I've got an idea, Midnight. A *brilliant* idea. Do you want to hear it?"

"No."

She just laughed. "I'm going to tell Wink you want to meet her tomorrow at midnight in the Roman Luck house. I'm going to tell her that you want to be alone with her, really alone, no Bell brats, no hayloft. I'm going to tell her you're too shy to ask her yourself."

"She won't believe you, Poppy."

"Yes she will. I'm a fantastic actress. I'll make her." Poppy laughed again, quiet, so my dad wouldn't hear. He was still awake, his footsteps making my ceiling creak. "It's going to be so beautiful. So *wicked*."

"No, it won't. It really won't."

"Yes, it *will*. When she gets there, I'm going to tie her to the grand piano and then leave her there. Alone. She'll have to spend the whole night sitting in the music room of the haunted Roman Luck house, with its ghosts. It's going to be amazing."

"Don't, Poppy. Please." I stopped trying to sound like Alabama. I just sounded like me again.

Poppy leaned forward and kissed the hollow of my throat. Slowly. "Will you help me do this? Will you go along with it?"

"No."

"Do it, Midnight. Help me."

"No. Never."

Her kisses were languid. Soft. Perfect.

"If you don't help me, Midnight, I'll do something worse."

Her lips, my skin . . .

Damn it, damn it, damn it.

"If you don't help me I'll set the hayloft on fire and burn the barn to the ground and say Wink did it. I'll say she's insane. I'll say she's dangerous. I'll say she's a liar. I'll say she lured me into the woods and tried to kill me. I'll say she pushed me in the river and tried to drown me. I'll say she—"

"All right, *all right*." I put my hand over her lips to stop her from kissing me again. "All right. I'll do it."

She raised her arms in the air and squealed. It was whispery and quiet, but still a squeal.

Even Poppy's squeals were sexy.

"But Poppy, you have to promise that after this you'll leave her alone. This is the last prank. The *last* one. Okay?"

Poppy crossed her arms over her bare chest, tossed her hair, and smiled. "I knew you'd come around."

"Promise me it will stop, Poppy."

Silence.

*"Promise."*

"It will stop. After this one last prank."

"And I don't want any Yellows there either. They'll make too much noise and she'll suspect something." I narrowed my eyes, back to imitating Alabama again. "Wink is smart. Smarter than you think. Just me and you on this, all right?"

*"Wow.* You're being so alpha and demanding tonight. I'm impressed. And I'm never impressed, especially by you."

She leaned in . . .

I put my hands on her shoulders and pushed her back.

She let out a cute, childish groan. *"Okay.* No Yellows and no more pranks."

She smiled again.

And then she slipped her left leg over me and sat her hips down on mine. "I wouldn't miss doing this with you for the world. Not for the world. Wink, Roman Luck, you and me, it's going to be so much fun, so much *fun*."

She bent forward until we were touching, chest to chest, skin to skin.

Lips. Down, down, down.

And I wanted to hate it.

I wanted it to turn my stomach, make me sick, fill me with horror. But it didn't.


# Poppy

I HID IT well, but climbing into Midnight's bed gave me a comforting feeling, a nostalgic feeling, like staying at my grandfather's cabin when I was little, back before he shoveled snow on a cold day seven years ago, had a heart attack, and died. His name was Anton Harvey and my parents used to leave me with him when they went away for their doctor conferences. My grandpa never once called me a *sweet little angel baby*. He hadn't given a damn about my blond halo hair or my big gray eyes or my cherub lips, and he never ever gave me pink presents with bows on them.

Anton Harvey was gruff and silent and he showed me how to gut fish after we caught them from the river, and he wasn't upset that I liked it. I wore flannel shirts when I stayed at his cabin, and Wellingtons, and I wore my hair in braids, and sometimes we went whole hours at a time without talking, just fishing or following tracks in the snow or sitting on the plain, tiny porch, watching a storm come in.

And just about the time I started to think, *Now here's something, here's someone I can actually look up to, he's not dumb dumb dumb like the rest, here's someone I can actually admire, someone I understand, someone I could probably even love, just give me half a chance*, he had to up and die.

## MIDNIGHT

"POPPY IS PLANNING something, Wink."

We were outside, cupped hands, drinking ice-cold water straight from the red water pump.

"I know." Wink cutely slurped up the water from her palms. "She was here earlier this morning. She found me in the hayloft and said you wanted to meet me at the Roman Luck house at midnight."

Poppy worked fast. Once she made up her mind about something she shot forward like a greyhound. She'd always been like this. The first time we'd slept together, she was already half-naked by the time she burst through my bedroom door.

"Poppy thinks I'm very, very stupid." Wink's eyes were extra green in the morning sunshine, and there were tiny drops of water on her lips.

The Orphans were all at the dentist. Wink said Mim didn't trust dentists but she brought them anyway. I could hear Dad through the open attic windows, all the way across the road, talking on the phone to one of his clients. He used rare book words that were so foreign and frequent it was almost another language.

"She wants to tie you to that old piano and leave you in the house overnight." I took my thumb and brushed the water droplets off her top lip, and she smiled at me when I did it. "Apparently Leaf told her you're afraid of the place."

Wink shook her head. "Leaf never told her that."

"So you aren't scared of the Roman Luck house?"

"Everyone should be scared of the Roman Luck house." A goat wandered up and butted its head against her legs and she ran her hand down its furry back.

As I said, getting straight info out of Wink was harder than getting kindness out of Poppy.

Wink kept her hand on the goat, but put her eyes on mine. "You know how Thief has a vision about the path he must take through the Dark Woods? The path that leads him to the beautiful magician in the secret cottage with the melancholy blue eyes and silvery hair?"

I nodded.

"Remember how the magician tries to trick him but he tricks her instead?"

I nodded again. "And then he leaves her body in the woods, knowing the wolves will get it come nightfall."

"Exactly." And then Wink fluttered the ends of her fingers in that way I liked.

Poppy was planning to trick Wink, and Wink was planning to trick Poppy, and I was stuck right in the middle.

But the air was hot and there was a nice breeze, and I somehow felt kind of dreamy and peaceful, despite everything. Wink did that to me.

That afternoon we drank coffee from the blue cup, dirt from the garden between our toes. We sat under the apple trees in my orchard, wide sky, fat clouds, fingers tickling the cold water in the tiny curving creek, twelve inches wide at most. I asked Wink the name of the stream and she said it didn't have one but that it came from the Blue Twist River and so she called it the Little Blue Twist.

"I've always wanted to have my very own creek," I said. "I'm sorry it turns south before it gets to your farm—I feel like I'm hogging it."

"It's okay. I want you to have the creek." She grinned at me. Her fingers looked pale and eerie white underneath the water. "Do you know what water witching is, Midnight? My pa could do it. I watched him once."

I looked at her, surprised. She'd dodged every question I'd asked about her father so far. Every single one. And now here she was, offering him up freely.

"Some people are born with the ability to find water underground." Wink leaned forward, and the tips of her hair dipped into the stream. "I once watched Pa find a buried spring in the pasture near the Gold Apple Mine, where we keep the horses. He held a forked stick and it started twitching really quick and fast. And that's how he knew. Someday I plan to gather all the Orphans and dig in that spot until the water bubbles up. And then we'll have a swimming pond."

"Why don't we do it today, Wink? I'd like to dig up a spring. I'd like to free it from deep underground."

Wink shrugged. "It's too hot. Not today, Midnight. Soon, though."

We went inside to get out of the sun. I showed Wink around my house, the airy kitchen with the white, tiled walls, the sleeping porch with all the screens, the basement full of Mom and Alabama boxes, the cellar with the dirt walls and empty jars.

I showed her my bedroom, and she looked at all the books

in my bookcases, all of them. Then she went over and sat on my bed. I flinched, worried that the pillows smelled like jasmine. She curled her legs underneath her, picked up the copy of *Will and the Black Caravans* I'd left open, and just set it in her lap. Wink had loaned the book to me—she said she hadn't read it to the Orphans yet because she didn't want them to get any ideas. She didn't want it to stir their blood. And I understood. I was only half-done but Will and the red-haired boy-king Gabriel Stagg had already entered my dreams . . . the twisting, endless road, the knives in the dark, the feeling of restlessness.

"I've given it some thought and I think I know what happened to Roman Luck," Wink said, out of the blue.

I sat down beside her and didn't say anything, waiting for her to go on.

"I think Roman Luck decided that he'd done it all wrong, his whole life. He didn't want to be a doctor anymore, and he didn't want to live in a grand house. So he just walked out the door and left, and started over someplace else with nothing but the clothes on his back, determined to change his fate."

I thought about this for a while. "I like the idea of it, but people don't just leave their house and money and identity behind. They just don't. Well, except for the old woman from Paris that you told me about."

Wink folded her hands under her pointed little chin. "There was an heiress once named Guinevere Woolfe who disappeared without a trace one day, off into the foggy streets of London. She was finally found twenty years later, baking bread in a tiny French alpine town. She'd married a French pastry chef, and had grown fat and happy, and they'd had six lively children, all boys. No one in the town had the faintest idea that she was English, let alone that she was worth fifty million pounds."

"So what did Roman Luck do, after he disappeared? Did he become a world-famous illusionist and spend his life traveling to exotic locations, only to die a sudden death on the Orient Express after drinking a poisoned cup of coffee in the dinner car with a jealous former lover?"

This was a fantasy I'd had about myself, once upon a time. The details varied from year to year, generally involving more and more beautiful women as I got older.

Wink smiled, quick and soft and eyes half-closed. "I think Roman Luck hopped a train to some faraway place, and started off a stranger and ended up a hero. I think he killed monsters and saved innocents, and rescued a sad, lonely girl and made her happy. That's what I think happened to him."

She stood up, and put her hands in her deep overall pockets, and let her curly hair fall across her freckled cheeks. "You could be a hero, Midnight. You could be a hero like Thief, and Roman Luck."

"Alabama's the hero, not me," I said, open and honest because Wink made me feel like it was okay to be that way.

"I'll help you. You can do it, you'll see." Wink nodded. It was a very serious and grave kind of nod. Her eyes were looking up to me, full of stars.

I heard tires on gravel. Car doors slammed. And then screams, kid screams, half laughter, half squeal. I got up and went to my window. The Orphans were back from the dentist and full of energy from being cooped up all morning. Peach was standing on top of the rusty Bell station wagon, messy hair down her back, trying to sing opera in her little voice. Felix had Bee Lee on his shoulders and was tickling her feet while she laughed hysterically. The twins were just running in circles around everyone else, like they couldn't make up their mind on what mischief to start first.

# WINK

WE WERE LIKE the three Fates, weaving the story together, threads of gold, red, and midnight blue.

There would be wolves and tricks and lies and cunning and vengeance in our story. I would make sure of it.

Long, long ago there lived a German storyteller who wove dark tales in a cottage hidden in the Black Forest. Pa told me about him. He said his books were burned in the Great War, and only a few survived, and someday he would let me read one.

Pa said this German storyteller had a recurring theme in all his tales, and he used to sing it to me in a low, sad voice, like it was a lullaby, over and over:

*When you look into the darkness,*

*the darkness looks into you.*

I mentioned my father to the Hero. I didn't mean to. I'd wanted to talk about the Huntsman, about how he cut out Sweet Ruby's heart, and put it in a box and gave it to the queen . . . but Pa slipped out instead, slipped right out of my mouth like the Crawly Eels, slipping in and out of the people's windows in *The City Beneath*.

I'd been thinking about Heroes, and Midnight, and how Leaf

used to say the best Heroes had a bit of evil in them, to make the good shine all the more for being next to it . . . and then the next thing I knew I was talking about *him,* and his water witching, and the Gold Apple Mine, like the little girl in *Winter Earnest* who had her wits knocked out of her all in one go.

I'd be more careful from now on.

# PoPpy

THE TENTH TIME I kissed Leaf, he kissed me back. We were in the meadow behind the Bell farm and his thin lips were tender and arrogant, exactly, exactly how I thought they would be, exactly how I wanted them to be, he pulled away and groaned against my cheek and that dark, empty part in my chest where my heart had never been, it started beating, beating, beating and I felt joy, red and dripping. He picked me up and turned me over so my back pressed into the grass and the bright little wildflowers, and my fresh new heart faced the sky.

Leaf had a low, growly kind of voice. I saw him singing once. Back before the Blue Twist River flooding, back before DeeDee, he must have been fourteen or fifteen, but not younger, because his voice had changed, and gotten deep. I saw him singing in the forest, I was out there by myself because being better than everyone at everything is really fucking tiresome, and sometimes I have to run off into the woods for a while and pretend no one else exists.

He was standing alone in a little clearing, snow-covered ground and crisp blue winter sky. His chest was puffed out and his head was thrown back and he was singing, just singing at the top of his lungs, some melancholy tune I'd never heard before. It sounded ancient, sung in his gravelly voice, old stone mountains and ice-cold lakes. His breath fogged up in the air and I'd never heard or seen anything half so fucking beautiful. He didn't see me, or pretended he didn't. He just kept singing.

I wasn't built for missing things, I was built for winning and getting what I wanted and not for trying to be better, not for trying to be the best version of myself, it wasn't working anyway, *god*, it wasn't working at all.

I had Midnight eating out of the palm of my hand, it was all so easy, so ridiculously easy. I was barely trying. He thought he was going to betray me, as if I'd let him, as if he had the cunning, what a notion, as if, as if.

This is how far I'll go, this is how far I'm willing to go.

# MIDNIGHT

WINK AND I walked through black trees to the Roman Luck house. It was ten thirty, maybe a quarter to eleven. I told Poppy I would show up at eleven thirty, and Wink and I needed to beat her there.

I shined the flashlight on the sagging porch.

I didn't like going in the Roman Luck house in the broad summer daylight. No one did. And now, in the dark . . .

The trees seemed to be watching us, watching me and Wink, all their rustling leaves like little eyes, blinking.

Maybe this was a bad idea.

Maybe this wasn't what Thief would do.

But then, Thief had a sword.

All I had was an abandoned house.

Wink's fingers crawled into mine. She squeezed. "You're the hero, Midnight."

We walked up the worn wooden steps together.

I turned the cold glass doorknob, and shoved.

The floor creaked as I stepped on it, just like the floors did in my own house. And it made me feel better. We walked down the narrow hallway, framed photographs still on the walls, fuzzy in the dim light, the faces of strangers, the faces of the people Roman Luck had run away from.

We ignored the dining room on our right, dusty table and chairs and a dirty plate that sat alone on one end, still untouched by everyone somehow, cops and kids alike.

The music room was next, on the left.

There were scurrying sounds coming from the corners. I ran my hand down the wall, and felt the velvet flowered wallpaper pucker under my palm. The faded red curtains were pushed back, floor to ceiling, framing the jagged edges of the broken bay window.

A cloud moved, and a sliver of moonlight flickered in. Chunks of plaster on the floor, a cushion on the piano stool, a heavy Rachmaninoff book of sheet music on the stand.

"Roman Luck must have played this piano sometimes." I nodded at the music. "Can't you just see him, sitting in this big house all by himself, playing dark Russian songs?"

"I can," she said. "I really can."

I set my backpack down on the floor. It held the rope, and another flashlight. I looked up at Wink, but she still hadn't moved. She was staring at the spot right between the piano and the ratty green sofa.

"It was right there," Wink whispered. "That's right where I saw him."

# WINK

I DIDN'T DUST my skin with sugar this time. I needed something more powerful. I was wearing my acorn skirt, the one with the sand from the bottom of the Blue Twist sewn into the hem for protection.

I filled one of the pockets with dried, dusky green lentils, and the other with cinnamon sticks from a jar in Mim's charm cupboard. I hung a key around my neck on a silver chain, the long skeleton one that the tiny lady in the black dress gave me when I stumbled upon her in the woods that one day. She said the key opened a golden box that contained the heart of a girl she'd killed years ago.

I knew I'd have to tell Midnight about the unforgivables now. I needed to warn him about how they feed on you if you're not careful, how they'll turn your heart into red dust and make you go hatter-mad.

# MIDNIGHT

"I WAS LITTLE," Wink said, voice soft, eyes staring down at the rotting Roman Luck floorboards. "As little as Bee Lee. Leaf was the same age as the twins. We were playing in the woods, a game that Leaf made up called Follow the Screams. I was hiding in a dead tree trunk and listening, and that's when I heard them, real screams, not Leaf-screams, coming from the Roman Luck house."

We had some time before Poppy showed up. She wasn't a ten-minute-early kind of girl. I was sitting on the green velveteen sofa, and Wink was sitting next to me, our knees touching. She was wearing a skirt with little acorns all over it. I held the flashlight in my hand, the light toward our toes.

The wind picked up outside. Branches scraped the broken windows and it sounded like someone's fingernails clawing at the glass.

I slid closer to Wink, until our thighs were touching.

"Mim told me that a woman named Autumn used to live here. This was a long time ago, before Roman Luck. Autumn wasn't right in the head. She married the handsomest man in town, a man named Martin Lind, and they had four children, two boys, two girls. But as time went on Autumn became paranoid and suspicious, and she accused her husband of being in love with another woman. She thought he was going to leave her."

Wink paused. She was rubbing the hem of her skirt between two fingers, and not looking at me.

"And then one day Autumn stabbed Martin in the stomach with a kitchen knife and left him in the music room to die."

I looked at Wink, looked at her innocent green eyes and her earnest, heart-shaped face. "Is that really true, Wink?"

She smiled suddenly, soft lips, cute ears. "You keep asking me that. Of course it's true. All the strangest things are true. Autumn hanged for it, *hanged by the neck until dead,* and her children grew up with strangers, orphaned and alone like in one of my hayloft stories. The house went up for sale, and Roman Luck bought it. But Autumn's bad thing, her unforgivable thing, had soaked into the floorboards, and creeped into the walls."

"You told me Roman didn't leave because of a ghost."

She shrugged. "Mim said he didn't. She read his cards sometimes, so she would know. Sometimes people just . . . leave."

An owl hooted somewhere out in the night. The hoo-hooing swept right through the broken glass, right into my ears, like a whisper from Poppy.

"I was hiding and I heard the screams and I went closer to see. There was a man in this room, Midnight, and he was screaming, and bleeding. He was dying. He was handsome, and beautiful, like a prince in a fairy tale. He didn't see me, not at first. I was little, and had to stand on my tiptoes, and I could still barely reach the windowsill. He was all in shadow and kept clutching his side and saying something, over and over."

Wink was using her Putting the Orphans to Sleep voice. But I wasn't getting sleepy this time.

"What?" I asked, when she didn't continue. "What did he say?"

*"Tell my children I love them.* That's what he said, again and again. And oh, Midnight, his voice was so raw and sad."

I looked around the room, and then slammed my eyes shut, thinking that the ghost of Martin Lind was going to appear in front of me, bleeding and clutching and crying out in the dark.

Had Wink really seen that as a girl? What would that do to a little kid's head?

I didn't even believe in ghosts, not really. But I did believe in Wink.

"I got scared then, and lost my footing," she said, still using her soft, sleepy voice. "I stumbled, and when I stood up again he was gone and the music room was empty. There is a ghost here, Midnight. But he didn't have anything to do with Roman."

The owl hooted. The branches scratched. The sounds scurried. The room smelled like night and dirt and neglect.

Wink leaned over and put her mouth on mine. I dropped the flashlight, clunk, creak. Her red hair fell over my ears and neck and shoulders.

She smelled like cinnamon, and her lips tasted like dust.

I didn't think about the man who had died in this room.

Or the unforgivable thing that Autumn had done.

Or what I was about to do to a girl I'd once loved.

I just thought about Wink.

She pulled away. Stood up, smoothed her acorn skirt. Her hair was tangled and beautiful and red, red, red in the flashlight's beam. "You can do this," she said. "You're Thief. You're the hero."

I nodded.

I nodded even though this didn't feel heroic.

It just felt wrong.

Wink left. Into the woods to wait.

Tick-tock, tick-tock.

Poppy arrived.

# POPPY

I WALKED OUT my front door at eleven, boldly, with a swagger, my parents were gone anyway, off to rub elbows in Chicago with other doctors at some boring convention, I could just picture them in a long carpeted room, expensive furnishings and chandeliers, looking smug and overly educated and really fucking proud of themselves.

I ran away once, after Grandpa died. I went to his cabin up on Three Death Jack Mountain and stayed there for two days, not giving a thought to my parents or anyone else. It was beautiful and quiet, so quiet. The cabin was kind of run-down by then, but I did what I could to fix it up and I was having the time of my life, catching fish and not talking to anyone, when Mom and Dad finally found me. They were panicked and angry, they just couldn't understand why I'd run off, why I'd want to live in some rat-hole cabin instead of our nice house in town, they gave me everything I wanted, hadn't they given me everything I'd ever wanted?

They burned Anton Harvey's cabin to the ground. They said it was falling apart and dangerous, but I knew. I knew why they really did it.

I took the cobblestone street to the cemetery, then down the path, into the woods. I wasn't scared of this part, I'd done it enough times. Owls hooting and things rustling around in dead leaves and the wind tickling my neck like the night was letting out its breath. But my sense of direction was far above average, and besides, what in the forest could possibly be scarier than me?

The Roman Luck house.

That was scarier, true, true, I hated that place, oh, how I hated it, but it was just one night, one quick night, close your eyes and think of England.

I HEARD THE Wolf before I saw her. She strolled into the clearing, kicking up dead leaves, chin up, back straight, vain as the Raven Queen.

I hid in the trees. I wasn't afraid of the dark. I was only afraid of the Roman Luck house. I didn't want to leave Midnight in there alone, even if he was the Hero.

I think he believed me, about the unforgivables.

# MIDNIGHT

POPPY STOOD IN the Roman Luck doorway, up on her tiptoes, trying to look over my shoulder.

"Wink isn't here yet," I said. "We still have ten or fifteen minutes."

She put her hands on the waist of her black skirt, right where it met her tight black T-shirt. I stepped back to let her enter, but she didn't move from the doorway.

"Are you still afraid of this place, Poppy?"

She was quiet. Poppy, without a comeback.

"Why did you choose it for the prank, then? Why here, if it scares you as much as Wink?"

Poppy shook herself, so quick I almost missed it. She cocked her head, eyes hooded, nose in air. "I chose this place because it's isolated. I'm not *afraid*. This is just a stupid, dirty old house that smells like death. I don't believe in ghosts and even if I did, I wouldn't care if I saw one and I wouldn't be afraid."

She tossed her blond hair and took a step. Then another. She was in.

She laughed.

Poppy held out her arms in the Roman Luck hallway, wide.

She twirled around in a circle, the floor creaking beneath her. "Come and haunt me, ghosts. I'm right here. Come *on*. Show me you're real. Show me what you can do."

She paused. Smiled at me. "See? Nothing."

She looked so young, right there with her arms spread out between the two wood-paneled walls. She looked so brave and full of life amid the groaning floorboards and the dust and decay that I felt, just for a brief second, like she could make it all vanish, just with a wave of her hand, a blink of her eye, a flash of light. Poppy would twirl her arm above her head and the house would lift itself up and shake off its dirt and squeeze itself back together and be like new again. And then Roman Luck would come strolling back through the door, stroking a long beard because he'd tasted some Dutch ale and fallen asleep on the mountain for twenty years, and that's all it was, that's all that had happened, mystery solved.

We both heard the noise, and jumped. Clawing, scratching, scrape, scrape, scrape.

Poppy dropped her arms.

It was just the branches rubbing up against the windows, but Poppy didn't know that.

I nodded down the hall. "Come on, let's go to the music room. Lead the way."

She didn't say anything, no snappy retort. She just went.

*Creak-creak* went the floorboards.

Poppy stopped in the doorway. I gave her my flashlight, and she switched it on. She walked to the center of the room, and then spun around, the light going with her. It made a long, pale arc. Poppy shivered. Hard. Her limbs shook.

This wasn't the Poppy I knew. It wasn't even the Poppy from the hallway, arms in the air, daring the supernatural to come and get her.

She wasn't being mean. She wasn't hurting someone. She wasn't ordering anyone around. She wasn't getting naked and climbing on top of me.

She was just scared. She was genuinely scared.

I wanted to take her hand and lead her back outside. I wanted to walk her home, and tuck her into bed, and make her feel safe.

But I couldn't.

I was the hero.

"You should put your hands on the keys," I said. "It's tradition. The first time you go in the Roman Luck house, you put your hands on the keys."

Poppy walked to the piano. She set down the flashlight, put her fingers on the chipped ivory, and pressed, *plunk, plunk, plunk.* She rested them there for one breath, two. Then snatched her arms away, turned back to me, and smiled a cocky half smile.

"There, I did it."

"You know," I said, lazy and cool, like Alabama, "I think you should call out to the ghosts again, here in the music room. Dare them to haunt you. See what happens."

"You first," she said, but the words didn't come out bossy and vain. They came out as a whisper.

Poppy hugged her arms across her chest and didn't look me in the eye.

"Well, you should at least go upstairs and lie down on the bed. That's the way it's done. Piano keys. Bed." I reached out my hand. She hesitated. I wiggled my fingers. "I'll go with you."

Out into the hall, up the stairs, first door on the right. The master bedroom. Seven black suits in the wardrobe. Two wooden nightstands. White radiator. A dusty tie on a dusty walnut dresser. And the bed, sheets still tucked in, covers still pulled up, even after all of us kids had been on it through the years. The striped black-and-gold quilt was spitting out stuffing from where the rats had gotten into it, but you could still tell it was silk. Still see the *Made in Paris, France,* tag when you flipped over the bottom right corner.

"Lie down on it." I'd never ordered Poppy to do anything before. Not once. Not ever. But she obeyed.

Her body slid across the silk, stretched out, hands and feet to the corners, blond hair spreading out beneath her head, like a girl about to be sacrificed, like the girl in one of Wink's hayloft stories, like Norah in *Sea and Burn*, stripped and chained to the rock, blond hair blowing in the wind, feet bare in the cold, waiting for dawn, waiting for the scaly beast to come out of the cave, and burn her alive. . .

Wink was having an effect on me.

I never used to think like this.

And I wasn't sure if I liked it or not.

I went over to Poppy.

I kissed the soft, translucent skin on the inside of her wrists.

My lips followed the blue veins as they ran toward her elbows.

Poppy sucked in her breath . . . held it . . .

And then burst out of my arms. She ran toward the door, and stood there, shivering, shoulders shaking and her chin trembling.

Her body slid down the doorframe until she was crouching, her bare knees popping out of her black skirt, her hands on her cheeks.

A knock on the door.

We both jerked.

She looked up at me.

"Go to the music room and hide," I whispered. "At least until I'm done tying her up. All right?"

Poppy nodded and left, though she didn't look happy about it.

It had been her idea to do this, to come here at night, to a place of ghosts and unforgivables. And so I wasn't going to feel bad for her.

I *wasn't*.

I waited ten seconds and then went down the stairs and opened the front door. Wink, pale face shining in the dark. She gave me a look, and I gave her a look. She nodded. I nodded back.

"Wink," I said, loudly, so Poppy could hear.

I led her into the music room, my arm around her little waist, my lips by her ear, playing the part.

Past the sagging wallpaper, past the green sofa.

Up to the grand piano.

I leaned Wink against it, and the Rachmaninoff pages fluttered. The piano made a deep, guttural sound, like pedals shifting and wires stretching. But it didn't budge.

I kissed her. I kissed her to keep up the ruse. I kissed her so Poppy would see. I wanted her to see. I slid my hands up Wink's back to the base of her neck. She leaned her head into my palms.

I took my time.

"Here we go," I whispered in Wink's ear. And felt her head nod against my cheek.

"Wink, I want you to close your eyes," I said, out loud. "And keep them closed. I have a present for you."

"Okay," she said, softly, softly.

I pulled my arms away, and Wink stayed where she was, head back, tips of her red hair touching the top of the piano.

I glanced toward the corner by the bay window, quick. I couldn't see Poppy, not even a faint outline. But I knew she was there.

I thought about the scurrying sounds I'd heard earlier, and hoped the rats were crawling over her feet and licking her ankles.

And then I felt bad for thinking that.

I kneeled down and got the rope out of the backpack.

I looped it around Wink's wrists, quick, and snapped it tight.

Her eyes flew open.

"What are you doing, Midnight?" And her voice was perfect. Small and apprehensive and starting to get scared. "What is this? What are you doing?"

"I'm tying you to the grand piano," I answered, nice and easy. "I'm going to leave you here by yourself, all night long." I looped the other end of the rope around the piano leg and pulled. Wink's arms flew out and she fell to her knees.

She started to cry, quiet, then louder.

"Why, Midnight, why? Why? *Why?*"

The Bells never cried. That was the thing about them. If Poppy had ever paid any attention, she would have guessed. She would have known.

But, instead, she laughed. She laughed, and then came running out of the corner. She laughed and pointed and practically danced with glee. She was supposed to stay hidden, but she just couldn't help herself.

And I'd counted on this.

"Feral Bell, tied to a piano, spending the night with the ghosts. Serves you right. Do you think the spirits will like your unicorn underwear? Do you? I can't wait to tell the Yellows about this. They are going to *die*." Laugh, laugh, laugh.

I gave it a second. Wink's performance was flawless. I wanted to keep watching. I couldn't help but keep watching.

Wink shrunk back, away from Poppy, pulling at the rope and scuttling along the floor like she'd been kicked. She curled herself into a ball, her knees under her chin, arms above her head, tangled red hair. Her green eyes glowed in the flashlight's beam, and they were *wild*. Wild, wild. Her lips drew tight, sucked in between her teeth.

"You'll regret it, you'll regret it." Her voice was high and clear, and I could barely recognize Wink in it at all. "They'll come for you. They'll find you. They'll slice you open and lap up all your blood, lap lap it up like a cat with milk . . ."

Poppy wasn't laughing anymore.

Wink coughed and coughed, and her whole body shook, legs and head and hands.

Then she went still again.

"The unforgivables are so hungry, so hungry . . ." Her eyes darted to the corner of the room, then shot back, and something in them was . . . wrong . . . so wrong . . .

Goose bumps up my spine, into my scalp.

"They . . . they want to open your head, pop it open, pop pop Poppy, dig out all its little secrets, wriggling, wriggling like maggots, dig them out and crush them, squish, squish, pop . . ."

Wink's voice got softer and softer.

"They told me things about you, Poppy. Come closer . . . come closer and I'll tell you what they said. You want to know, you need to know . . ."

Poppy went to Wink. She went right to her, step, step, step, creak, creak, creak. She leaned down . . .

And Wink shot forward.

She grabbed Poppy's arm, squeezing until her knuckles went white.

"Take her other arm," she said, calm, calm.

I took it. I wrapped my fingers around the elbow I'd been kissing earlier, upstairs. I did it even though it made me feel sick. Weak and sick, deep inside.

Wink was stronger than she looked. She bent Poppy's arm behind her and shoved it up hard against her spine. I wound the rope around one wrist, then the other, quick, before Poppy could fight back. I pulled . . .

But it was Wink who pushed Poppy to her knees. Wink who tied the knots, three deep and so hard Poppy's hands were smashed up against the piano leg.

Poppy looked up at me. One long, comprehending look.

And then she screamed.

I'd counted on this too.

"There's no one to hear you," I said. "You can holler your heart out and no one will hear you."

And I kind of felt like crying, after I said that. Just a little bit.

Poppy stopped screaming and started sobbing instead. It was messy and loud, full of tears and chokes and sobs.

"How can you? How can you leave me here?" Her big gray eyes were staring and pleading, lashes wet and shadow-black. *"You know how afraid I am.* Midnight, *please."*

I looked from Poppy, to Wink, to Poppy, to Wink.

I couldn't do this.

Wink would say I wasn't the hero.

And Poppy would say I was a coward. If I let her free she would call me a coward for it later. I knew she would.

But . . .

I reached in my pocket and got out my jackknife. I flipped it open and grabbed the rope—

Wink stepped in front of me, both hands up, like I held a gun.

"She's not Poppy. She's The Thing in the Deep. And you just struck her with your sword. She's the monster and you're the hero. This part of the story is over, Midnight. It's time to go."

She reached her small freckled fingers out to me.

And I took them.

We stood there facing the monster, side by side and hand in hand.

"I love you," Poppy whispered. She choked, sucked back a sob, and then said it again. "I love you, Midnight."

Tears slipped off the tiny crook in her nose, down her perfect chin, down her slender neck. Strands of blond hair stuck to her cheeks. She looked helpless, her arms in the air, her face wet, her eyes wide and scared. She looked young. Young as Bee Lee. Younger.

She said it again. *"I love you, Midnight."*

I shook my head. And I did it with my chin held high and my knife in my hand. "No, Poppy. You never did. You never, ever did."

And we left.

# Poppy

THE DARK. It was thick as drying blood, so thick I could have held it in my hands, if they were free, palms filled with it. I could feel the blackness breathing, panting, panting, the dark, the dark, the dark.

Not much longer now, it wouldn't be much longer, my wrists were itching, burning, my arms were falling asleep, they felt dead, dead weights on the ends of my shoulders, but I wasn't going anywhere, not yet. The scratching sounds came and went with the breeze, the breeze cleared the air, leaves and dirt and dew covering up the dust and dank and death, and I drew it in, sucked it in, like it was meant for me, like it would save me.

I screamed again. Scream, scream, scream. I was losing my voice, but it blocked out the dark, and the scratching, and the whispering, when had the whispering started? Had it always been there? Whisper, whisper, words I didn't know, stupid words, lumpy words, swampy words, the unforgivables, Wink made them up, I knew she did, I'd known all along, but then *who was whispering?*

My wrists hurt, my heart hurt, it was beating so fast, so fast, I couldn't keep up, *Leaf was whispering to me, we were in the meadow, and I was beside him on the grass and he was whispering, whispering that I was ugly on the inside, but he was kissing my wrists anyway, kissing them hard, so hard they were burning from it, burning up, and my arms were wrapped around him, so tight they were going numb and this was why, this was why, whispers and heartbeats, whispers and heartbeats, all around me. I wanted to put my hands over my ears but I couldn't, the whispers drew in closer, so close they were touching me, inside me, through my skin, into my insides, into my inner deeps, I couldn't bear it, I couldn't bear one more second of it . . .*

I screamed. And screamed.

I tried to keep counting, counting my own flashing heartbeats, just to make sure, one two three, one two three . . .

But then, just like that, like a door slamming in the wind . . .

Everything went quiet.

Everything, for once, was quiet.

I COULD HEAR her screaming. We were half a mile away from the Roman Luck house and I could still hear. Midnight could too, he tensed each time. I felt it.

Bad people still put out traps in the woods. Leaf and I found a coyote once, his back foot caught in the metal teeth. The coyote screamed and screamed. He tried to bite Leaf, and did, on his upper arm, a deep nip, but Leaf got him free all the same. The coyote ran off on his three good feet and didn't look back.

Leaf stayed out in the forest for two days straight, waiting for the trap man to return to his snare. When Leaf finally came home the front of his shirt was dripping blood. Mim didn't ask questions. She never asked Leaf questions.

I see the coyote sometimes, standing in the trees at the edge of the farm, looking at me with his big ears and bushy tail. I know it's him, because of the limp. He watches us for a while, and then retreats into the woods, back to doing his coyote things. He's looking for Leaf, but I don't know how to tell him that Leaf is gone.

I'd put out a trap in the woods.

I'd caught a wolf.

And now it was screaming.

If Poppy was the Wolf, and Midnight was the Hero . . .

Then who was I?

# MIDNIGHT

WE WERE GOING to leave her for an hour.

Just an hour.

Wink said that's how long it would take. At least an hour, to kill a monster. We went to the hayloft and she gave me a cup of Earl Grey and read the leaves after I'd sipped it all. She held the cup in her hands, elbows sticking out, and said my leaves spoke of witches and beasts and princes.

It started raining, soft at first, then harder and harder, thunder snapping across the sky.

I asked Wink about what she'd said, when she'd been tied up. About the hungry unforgivables and the lapping up the blood and the popping open Poppy's brain.

"Where did you come up with all that, Wink? I believed it. I was scared of you. I was."

Wink smiled, and her ears popped out. "Sometimes I put on plays with the Orphans. Hops and Moon love madmen. They want all our plays to have madmen in them, so I usually play a character that's wandering a barren moor or locked up and screaming in a dungeon, or a tower, or an attic. I've gotten pretty good at it. Mim says we shouldn't pretend to be mad people, she thinks it draws bad spirits . . ."

Wink shrugged, then pointed up at the ceiling. "I string up a curtain between the beams here in the hayloft to make a stage. Peach wants to play all the roles and Bee Lee doesn't want to play any and Hops and Moon laugh right through all their lines. It's fun."

I sighed, my arms beneath my head, my body feeling heavy in the hay.

I tried not to think about her. Poppy. Out there in the house. Alone. Scared.

I was here with Wink in the hayloft. Exactly where I wanted to be.

As if she could read my mind, Wink came over and cuddled hard into my side. She started talking about Thief. About how he wasn't just another boy with a sword on a journey. She talked about how he walked through the Hill Creeps, and didn't go insane, and only the bravest could do such a thing. She talked about the first time he saw Trill, how she was running from the black Witch Wolves, long white veil streaming behind her, bare feet making small dents in the snow.

Wink put her hand up the back of my shirt, and ran it up my spine, up and down, up and down, up and down, softly, softly, slowly, slowly, and it was making me sleepy . . .

I stretched in the hay and sighed.

I kept an eye on the hayloft opening, on the night sky,

trying to tell time by the moon like you do with the sun . . .

*Poppy screaming. Poppy crying. Pulling at the rope, wrists bleeding, Roman Luck standing next to her, looking lost, Martin Lind collapsed on the floor, groaning about his children, rats running over his body, Wink opening the book,* The Thing in the Deep, *showing it to me, showing me how Thief had changed, how he looked different now, how he had shifty eyes, and slouched shoulders, and straggly hair . . .*

I opened my eyes.

Closed them.

Open. Close. Open.

I'd fallen asleep.

I'd fallen *asleep.*

"How long has it been, Wink? How long since we left her?"

Wink yawned. Her head was under my chin and her arms nestled into my chest. "I don't know. I fell asleep too."

I looked outside.

It was still dark, but dawn was coming. I could see it on the horizon, clawing at the night.

WINK PULLED AN apple out of one of her deep pockets and we shared it on the way there. I didn't feel like eating, but I just kept taking bites, hoping the crisp, familiar taste would make me feel normal again.

The path was wet from the storm, and my shoes sunk into mud and old pine needles.

I wanted to run to Poppy, run like something was chasing me, like one of Wink's Witch Wolves had its teeth at my heels, heart thudding, sweating, panting, wind on my cheeks.

*Why wasn't I running?*

I wanted to cut her free, and tell her I was sorry, so, so sorry. I wanted it so much I could *feel* my fingers on the rope, the cold metal of my knife, her messy blond hair, her look of relief . . .

But my steps got slower and slower, the closer we got.

The apple was tart and juicy and this felt real.

*This.*

Walking with Wink, the apple, the fresh air.

Not before, in the house, with the scurrying sounds and Wink's unforgivables and Poppy, oh Poppy . . .

The Roman Luck mansard roof. There it was suddenly, peeking out between branches and leaves.

I stopped walking.

"Did I dream it?" I asked Wink. "Did I just dream it all up, what we did?"

She looked at me and shook her head. "No, Midnight." She took the apple, one last bite, and then threw it into the trees.

I couldn't go in. I stood on the broken, splintered steps, and couldn't go in.

It was lighter already. The sky was gray, not black.

I wondered how long Poppy had screamed before finally giving up.

I'd never get the sound of her screams out of my head, or my heart.

Is this what it meant to be the hero? Is this what Wink thought it meant?

I wondered if Poppy tried to chew her way through the rope. I wondered if she pulled at it until her wrists bled, like in my nightmare.

I wondered what kind of person she would be now.

I wondered what kind of person I would be now.

Wink took my hand and pulled me through the Roman Luck door.

Down the hall.

Into the music room.

Poppy's arms were above her head, smooth and translucent in the murky dawn light. I could see the veins running down the inside of her elbows. Her right cheek rested against her shoulder. I couldn't see her eyes.

There was blood. Dried flakes of it on her chin, and down her neck.

"She must have cried so hard she bit her tongue," Wink whispered. Her voice was soft and calm and normal . . . but her face looked worried.

"Poppy," I called out, keeping my voice low, and strong, like a hero's. "Poppy, wake up. We're going to let you go. We're sorry we left you here all night, but you can leave now."

She didn't move. I took out my pocket knife, flipped it open. I stepped forward. The floor creaked.

No eyelids fluttering. No moaning. No squirming. Nothing.

I looked back over my shoulder at Wink. And she was . . . she was . . . she looked . . .

Wrong.

*Wrong.*

Wink ran forward. Down to her knees, her cheek on Poppy's chest, ear to her heart.

"The knife," she said. "Quick."

I cut the rope, hacked at it, hacked and hacked, *why had I used my knife to cut up all the cardboard moving boxes? Alabama had told me that cardboard would dull the blade—*

The rope snapped in two.

Poppy's arms dropped, heavy, like lead. Stone. Her skirt was pushed up and her hands smacked against her bare legs before hitting the floor.

Wink wrapped Poppy in her arms. She leaned her head against her shoulder, gently, gently.

I stopped breathing.

The edges of the room blurred.

Wink was staring at me. Her eyes seemed huge, big as saucers, like the dog in the story she read in the hayloft, the one about the tinderbox and the soldier.

Poppy moved. Just a little, just her lips.

*"Midnight."*

Her voice came quiet, like a thief in the night.

*"Midnight."*

Her eyelids fluttered . . .

I couldn't stand it, I couldn't stand looking at her. I didn't want to see what her eyes would say, once they opened . . .

I turned away and stared at the fluttering red curtains instead.

*"Midnight."*

The red curtains fluttered and fluttered. You could really see how dirty they were, in the dawn light. Sun-bleached, faded to pink in places and teeming with dust and grime. Flutter, flutter.

*"You didn't come back,"* she said. *"You left me here, and you didn't come back."*

I didn't look at Poppy. I didn't look at Wink. I just stared and stared at the red flutter flutter.

Flutter. Flutter.

I ran.

Down the hall and out the door and down the steps and into the woods.

I ran away.

Heroes didn't run away.

I wasn't a hero.

I turned and looked over my shoulder, and there was Wink, coming right after me, acorn skirt and freckles and saucer-green eyes.

She was fast. She caught up. She grabbed me and held me.

Her skin melted into mine, blood to blood, bone to bone. We hugged and melted into each other as the sun burst into the sky and the birds started singing.

"I have to go," Wink said. "I helped Poppy to the green sofa, but she's not well, Midnight. She didn't want me to leave her alone. You need to go back to her. Stay with her. I'm going to get Mim."

THE WOLF DIDN'T look like the Wolf anymore, tied to the piano with dried blood on her face.

She just looked like a girl named Poppy.

# MIDNIGHT

I DID IT. I went back.

The green sofa was a mess of blond hair and black skirt and long legs. I kneeled down. Her eyes were closed and I didn't know what to do at first, so I just took the corner of my shirt and wiped at the blood around her mouth.

"I can't move my arms," she said.

Her voice was hoarse, and raw, and soft. Her cheeks were pale and waxy, and her skin was cold, snow-cold, ice-cold.

"My hands are numb, so numb, Midnight. I can't move them at all."

I wanted to turn away and stare at the curtains again.

I wanted to run.

But I didn't. This time I didn't.

I started to rub her arms from shoulder to fingertips. I rubbed until my fingers ached, over and over and up and down, and *please move your arms again, Poppy.*

Finally, finally, her right hand twitched. And then her whole arm. And then she sat up and screamed. She cradled one arm in the other and just screamed.

Sometimes when I was a kid I'd lie the wrong way in bed

and my legs would go to sleep. I'd wake up in a panic, unable to move, convinced I'd lost my legs in a horrible accident. I'd shout out and Alabama would come running. He'd sit by me and tell me I was all right, just hang on, just hang on, until *boom,* the blood came roaring back. And it hurt, god, it hurt. I'd sit there and shake and pound my legs with my fists and Alabama would stay calm and cool and just keep telling me the pain was good, it meant everything was all right. He'd do this until I could move again. Until I could sleep again.

Poppy screamed and shook on the ratty green Roman sofa and I just kept telling her she was going to be all right, over and over again, like Alabama.

If I'd felt bad before, it was *nothing* to how bad I felt now.

*"You're going to be all right,"* I said. *"You're going to be all right."*

Finally, finally, her arms went slack in her lap, and she went still.

Poppy opened her eyes.

I looked into them. I made myself do it.

They were scared.

And hurt. So *hurt.* I hadn't known a person could look so hurt.

"You must all really hate me," she whispered, her voice quiet and scratchy like it was being dragged over gravel. "You must really, really hate me."

I didn't deny it. I couldn't.

It was true.

I'd hated her.

I felt sick suddenly. Sick like the flu, mixed with too little sleep and cold, clammy fear. The room started blurring at the edges, and I started seeing spots . . .

"Just leave me alone," Poppy whispered. "Go away, Midnight, and leave me alone."

And I did.

I ran out of the house. I ran out and left her there. Again, again, all over again.

I found Wink and Mim on the path.

Mim's red hair was in thick, tied-up braids and her long red skirt was swinging across the muddy path, turning the hem black.

They stopped walking and looked at me.

Mim was serene. Not anxious. Not confused. Not uneasy. Just serene. "You're very pale," she said, and gave me a mothering side eye.

"I left Poppy. I just left her in the house. I couldn't stand the look in her eyes. I . . ."

I blinked. Hard. *I'm not going to cry, I'm not going to let Wink see me cry, damn it.*

Mim just nodded. "Wink gave me a few details. A very few. How did this girl end up tied to the piano all night?"

Wink glanced at me and I glanced at her. I blinked again. And again.

"She just did," Wink said, finally.

Mim stared at us, sharp and wary now. She took her hands off her hips and held one out to me and the other out to Wink. "Give me your palms. Quick. Both of you."

I slid my fist onto Mim's strong, callused fingers, and opened it. Wink did the same. Mim leaned over my hand.

"Enough," she said, a second later, and dropped my palm.

She read Wink's next. Ten seconds. Twenty.

Wink looked up at her mother, and their eyes met, green to green. Something passed between them . . . a flicker—

"You went too far," Mim said, so quiet I almost didn't hear. She stared at Wink for another long second, dropped her hand, and started walking toward the Roman Luck house.

We followed behind.

Through the front door, down the hall, into the music room.

But we were too late.

Poppy was gone.

# WINK

MIM MOVED ABOUT the kitchen and made golden turmeric milk and never said a word.

I stood in the corner and watched her, but she never looked at me. Not once.

She was angry.

And Poppy was missing.

There was a hayloft book called *The Wolf Without a Howl*. It was about a white wolf that lost her entire pack to starvation one long, cold winter. Afterward, she was too sad and lonely to howl. It was a forlorn tale and I didn't read it to the Orphans very often.

We'd killed the monster, Midnight and I.

We'd taken the howl out of Poppy.

# MIDNIGHT

WINK SAT ON a hay bale, and I sat on the hayloft floor, my head against her skinny knees, her hands in my hair.

"Do you think Poppy just went home? I'm worried about her, Wink."

Wink made her little *hmmm* sound. "In *The Fairy Evil*, Jennie Slaughter was cast off by the Tree Fay and wandered the moors for three years, not remembering who she was or where she belonged. Maybe Poppy lost her mind and is wandering the woods like Jennie."

I moved my head, and her hands slid away. "I'll never forget seeing her there, with her wrists tied to the piano leg and the dried blood on her face and the bright blue veins running down her white arms. It's burned into my brain. Forever."

"I know what a dead person looks like," Wink said, after a while. "I know what a dead person *feels* like. I held Alexander, that day in the fog. Poppy was close to dying when we found her, Midnight. Her skin was cold and blue-tinted . . . she was clammy and stiff . . ."

"Who's Alexander?"

"No one."

"What day in the fog?"

Silence.

I got up and went to the hayloft opening. I stared down at the farm below, and watched Hops and Moon trying to climb the side of Wink's house using nothing but their hands and feet, like monkeys, while Peach alternately yelled out encouragement and criticism.

I sat back down and Wink ran her fingertips over my scalp. She smelled like cinnamon. "Mim knows we did it. She knows we tied her up and left her there."

Wink's fingers stopped moving. "Yes."

"Is she angry?"

"Yes."

I turned, so I could see her face.

The summer sun was bringing out Wink's freckles. They were darker than they had been just a few days ago. Her freckled skin was so different from Poppy's perfect milky white. And I liked it. I liked it so much it hurt.

"Wink, I'm scared that the night in the Roman Luck house *damaged* Poppy in some deep way. I don't think we did the right thing. I don't feel, in my heart, that it was right."

"She would have done the same to me, if you hadn't stopped her. Sometimes the only way to fight evil is with evil."

But I'd seen Poppy shivering and shivering and I'd still tied her up and left her in the Roman Luck house. And then I'd fallen asleep and not gone back to free her until dawn.

"You destroyed the monster, Midnight. That's what the hero does."

After Poppy, after all her lying and lying, I didn't believe anyone about much of anything anymore. Except Alabama, and he was in France.

But I *wanted* to believe Wink.

Her eyes met mine, and I saw a cloud pass over them, like she knew. Like she'd just read the doubt in my mind.

And then she hugged me, tight, her arms around my neck, her cheek in its hollow, her skin nuzzling into mine. She wound her fingers in my hair, and her freckles flowed around me like a scarf and she was whispering things in my ear, hero things, Thief things . . .

Bee Lee started climbing up the hayloft ladder. I knew it was her because she was singing a little song to herself about chickadees and werewolves. When she got inside she went right up to me, like she sensed something. She ran sticky fingers over the back of my hand and smiled at me.

"Are you okay, Midnight?"

I shook my head.

"I have bad days too." She pulled a strawberry out of her

pocket, plucked the green stem off, and gave it to me. "But tomorrow will be better. That's what Mim always says. You just have to eat a strawberry and then wait for tomorrow."

I WENT TO Poppy's house. I stood at the door for ten minutes, and never rang the bell.

It wasn't until I finally turned to leave that I saw Thomas lurking in the shadows near the lilac bushes, watching me.

He didn't say anything. I didn't say anything.

I ate supper with my dad, late, which he liked. Tomato, mozzarella, and pesto sandwiches, sitting on our front steps, facing the orchard and the creek and the Bell farm.

There were fireflies.

If I was extra silent and he knew something was wrong, he didn't ask me about it.

My bedroom smelled like jasmine. It hung on the air, thick and humid. I threw off my clothes and fell on the bed and closed my eyes and told myself it wasn't real. Poppy wasn't in my room. She'd never be in my room again. I'd seen to that.

I'd made my choice. I'd gotten my wish.

My mom used to make pumpkin hot chocolate every fall. She'd put milk, vanilla, cinnamon, maple syrup, and chocolate in a pan, and then when it was hot she'd whisk in a can of pumpkin puree. Alabama and I could drink whole mason jars of the stuff, and did. And now just the sound of my feet crunching on fallen leaves conjures up the smell of it, crystal clear, like I had a mug of it right in front of me.

The jasmine . . . it was like the pumpkin hot chocolate. It was all in my head.

But I dreamed of her anyway. I dreamed she came in through the window and lay down next to me, her silky blond hair spreading across my chest.

THE STORY HAD started in earnest now.

The threads were spinning.

Midnight was shook up. He destroyed the monster. That was always a turning point on the Hero's journey, like when Peter kills the wolf on the other side of the Wardrobe and the Lion tells him to clean his sword. Like when Elsbeth cuts out Jacob's heart, and roasts it on a spit, and feeds it to his lover, in *Elsbeth Ink and the Seven Forests*.

There are Scottish folktales that tell of people who go off into the Highlands, and disappear into the mist, and are never seen again.

That's what happened to Roman Luck.

That's what happened to my father. He disappeared into the mist. I thought he was the Hero, but he was just a man.

I told Midnight that I'd held Alexander in the fog the day he died. Alexander was the Hero in *A Cloak, A Dagger, A Journey*—but he'd been alone when the poison reached his heart, at the end. He fell down on the road, his hands clutching the golden penny whistle that the black-haired princess gave him the day he saved her life.

I'd imagined what it would have been like, imagined it so clearly, with the cold mist on my neck and his eyes going dark and his body going stiff in my arms. It was real. It happened.

Mim came into my room, later that night, after the Orphans were asleep. She asked me if there was anything I wanted to tell her.

I just shook my head and kept quiet.

## MIDNIGHT

I WAS STRETCHED out in my bed and staring at the windows. It was raining again. I stayed there so long Dad knocked on my door, a cup of green tea in his hand. I got up, took it, and slid back under my covers.

*Her body, slumped and blue in the gray light.*

*The look in her eyes.*

*Her screams when the blood came rushing back.*

I threw on a jacket and walked in the rain, into town. I went the long way around. I didn't want to go by the Roman Luck place. I couldn't.

I stood on her doorstep. Didn't ring the bell.

I'd done this the last two mornings.

"She's not there." Thomas stepped out of the shadows by the lilac bushes, wet blond hair sticking to his forehead. "She's missing. Her parents are gone at a medical conference and she's missing and no one is going to answer that door, Midnight."

My heart skipped a beat. Thomas hadn't seen Poppy either? I thought she'd been avoiding me, just me. "I need to talk to her, Thomas. Badly. I'm sure she's around somewhere. She's probably just down by the river. She likes to have picnics in the rain, bread and cheese and a bottle of wine and cold, fat raindrops on her cheeks."

"That was the first place I looked."

"She could be at the coffee shop, the one with the high ceilings and the caramel-colored lattes."

He shook his head.

"Or at the church—she likes to sit in a back pew and listen to the organist practice."

Thomas's eyes were red and he looked . . . smaller, somehow. Almost fragile. "She's gone. Disappeared. I was scared something like this might happen. That's why I've been watching her house."

"Something like what?" And my voice started high and went even higher at the end.

"Poppy's been sad lately. Really sad. Didn't you notice?"

"Poppy's not sad. She's never sad. She laughs at everything. That's the first thing I knew about her. She always just laughs."

This was a lie.

I'd seen her crying her eyes out, three nights ago.

Thomas shook his head, wet hair flying. "If you can't see past all that, past the way she brushes everything off to protect herself, then you don't deserve to know her.

"It's all an act, Midnight. It's an *act*. She's been perfecting it since she was a kid, and so she's really good at it, but it's just an act."

*Poppy, sobbing and screaming when she realized I was really going to leave her, all alone, in that house . . .*

How well had I known the girl I'd been sharing my bed with for a year?

Thomas started talking again. He was staring off toward the gazebo and rambling, like I wasn't even there.

". . . Briggs and his temper, the things he said, that last time he caught me and her together. Poppy just laughed them off, like always, but they were so mean, so *mean*. He said she was a liar and a spoiled brat. He said no one would ever really love her, and she didn't deserve love, she deserved to die alone. But no one deserves that, no one . . ."

Thomas put his hands over his eyes, and pressed. The rain started up again, and the drops hit his fingers and ran down his wrists and forearms. I zipped my jacket shut, and waited.

He moved his hands away from his face and looked at me, red, red eyes. "I'm scared Poppy might have run away. She did that once, last year. She was gone for three days. Did you know that?"

I did.

"We have to find her. We have to help her, Midnight."

"Okay," I said. "Okay, Thomas."

"So you'll help me? You'll help me look? I don't trust Briggs. I don't trust any of the other Yellows. I don't want them to know. They hate her. They follow her around, and do what she says, but they all hate her."

I looked at the wet grass, and the edges of the lawn blurred, a blurry green swirl. I felt sick again for a second. I put my hand on my heart and took deep breaths.

Was Thomas right?

*You must all really hate me,* she'd whispered to me there on the sofa in the Roman Luck house. *You must really, really hate me.*

"What don't you want the Yellows to know? That she's missing?"

"No, they already know she's missing. I don't want them to know about the letter." Thomas reached into the pocket of his hoodie and pulled out a black piece of paper. "I found this last night in our hiding spot. Mine and Poppy's. It was in the hollow of one of the Green William Cemetery trees. No one knows about it except us."

He handed it to me, and his eyes were kind of pleading.

I opened the letter, shielding it from the rain with my arm. Silver letters, silver on black:

> *I'm scared, Thomas, I'm scared of myself,*
> *I'm scared what I'll do.*
>> *When the time comes, I'll jump, I know*
> *I will.*
>> *Don't tell the other Yellows, they won't*
> *understand, tell Midnight, only Midnight.*
>> *Remember when we hiked up to Three*
> *Death Jack at night and watched the skiers*
> *on Mount Jasper and the ski lift was lit*
> *up like Christmas? We felt like Greek gods,*
> *sitting on Mount Olympus. You said I was*
> *a natural, laughing at all the mortals and*
> *their maudlin, trivial lives . . .*

*This life, my life . . .*
*It's not trivial.*
*It's . . .*
*Mine.*
*Mine, mine, mine.*

I held the paper up to my nose. It smelled like jasmine.

"It's a clue," Thomas said. "She meant it as a clue. We can use it to find her."

And there was something about the way he said that, something in his voice, that made me doubt.

I looked over my shoulder, all around Poppy's perfect green yard.

Nothing.

No one.

Was this another of Poppy's tricks? Like when she hid in the forest and made the Yellows stop us and demand that stupid kissing contest? Was she going to step out from behind one of the lilac bushes, laughing her head off at me for being so gullible? Was this her revenge for what Wink and I did to her? An elaborate setup with letters and clues and Yellows?

Or maybe that wasn't it. Not at all.

Maybe this wasn't about revenge.

Maybe it was something else entirely.

Thomas took the letter back, put it away, and looked up

at Poppy's bedroom window, the one that faced the street. "I have this feeling that if we don't find Poppy soon, we won't find her at all. I've read and read the letter, twenty times, a hundred times. What does it mean? What's the clue?"

I FOUND THE boy, the tall, dark-haired one with different-colored eyes, blue and green, one sky and the other sea. I was walking through the trees in the rain, thinking maybe I'd spot the solemn Strangers dancing to melancholy tunes in a woodland patch of dappled sun, like they did in *Wild Edric and the Londonderry Girl*. And that's when I saw him, rooting around in the wilderness behind the Roman Luck house.

He didn't seem surprised to find me standing beside him. He stared right through me almost, as if I wasn't there at all. He was on his knees, brushing away dirt and dead pine needles with his hands, acting kind of hatter-mad. He kept looking over his shoulder, as if the trees were hiding things behind their fat trunks, which maybe they were.

The dark-haired boy got to his feet and then picked something up from the ground where he'd just been kneeling. A shovel.

There wasn't a good reason to bring a shovel to the woods. There wasn't a *sane* reason. The Folk brought shovels to the woods and dug things up and put a glamor on them. They made the dug-up things look like the babies they'd stolen and were raising as their own. And sometimes the Folk returned and buried those stolen babies right back in the dirt, if they screamed too much and were not liked. But the dark-haired boy wasn't doing this. He wouldn't even know about it.

"Why are you digging?" I asked.

The rain had stopped, and the sun was poking out, and the dark-haired boy with the different-colored eyes nodded at me, kind of nicely.

"Poppy's disappeared," he said.

"A lot of people disappear," I said.

"I was horrible to her," he said. "Horrible, horrible. She thinks I hate her."

"No she doesn't," I said.

"She left a note," he said.

"Let me see it," I said.

And he put his dirty hands in his pockets and pulled out a black piece of paper with silver letters.

*Briggs.*

*Briggs, do you know how you gave me that marble once, the really big one with the gold*

*streak in the middle that you said you won
in a fight when you were a kid, and I made
fun of you for being into marbles, but you
just ignored me and said it matched my gold
hair, and I should have it?*

*We were in the woods drinking lemonade
out of teacups and I got sentimental
suddenly and told you to bury the marble
under that big pine between the two little
aspens so I'd always know where it was.*

*You hate me, Briggs. You all hate me,
and I deserve it. I deserve every ounce of it.*

*I wish I'd kept that gold marble. I wish
I had it now. Promise me you'll find it, you
have to promise, even if you're angry, even
though you hate me, promise you will.*

*Ask Midnight to help you look. He's
good at finding things.*

"Can I keep this?" I said, holding the letter up in the air, but
he was already gone. The boy with two different-colored eyes
walked off into the woods, tiny flecks of sun filtering through
the trees and sparking off his silver shovel. He went deep and
deeper, until he disappeared.

# Poppy

I only come out at night now, I walk through the woods and plop down on the pine needles, starlight covering me like a gauzy blanket.

I sneak into Midnight's room and he's such a deep sleeper, he doesn't even wake up when I put my lips on his.

I do all kinds of things after dark, some things I used to do but some new things too. I see everything. I spy on the Yellows and they never know I'm there. They couldn't see me if they tried, I'm so good at hiding, as good as it's possible to be. I was obvious before, loud and obvious, wanting all eyes on mine, needing it, look at me, worship me. But now no one ever sees me, and I like it, I like it. There's only one place I don't go, I don't go back to the Roman Luck house, I hate that place, hate it, hate it, hate it.

# Midnight

Bee Lee fell asleep leaning against my side while Wink read *The Thing in the Deep* in the hayloft after supper. Felix was with his new girlfriend in the garden, but Peach and the twins were listening quietly. It always surprised me how the three of them could be so wild and then settle down so quickly when Wink started a story.

I meant to tell Wink about Thomas, and the letter. But when I found her up in the hayloft with the Orphans, they were all looking so cuddly and happy, I couldn't do it.

Later.

Thief was at the Never-Ending Bridge over the River Slay. The old woman who guarded the bridge wouldn't let him pass until he played Five Lies, One Truth with her. In the end, all six were lies. Thief guessed right, and won, and the old woman screamed in rage and tore out her long, white hair.

*"The Never-Ending Bridge led to The Hill Creeps, where Thief would face his greatest trial. If he could pass through the hills and not go mad, then he would finally reach The Thing in the Deep. He would fight her, and kill her with the sword his father left him, and avenge his true love, Trill . . ."*

Wink's soft voice drifted up to the tall rafters of the hayloft and echoed back down again. It made me feel calm and peaceful and like everything was okay. Bee Lee had hay in her brown hair and I pulled it out, gently, so I wouldn't wake her. Her hand was in mine, but it went slack after she fell asleep.

Wink was using her Putting the Orphans to Sleep voice. I leaned against her side, as Bee leaned against mine. I reached up and moved a batch of red curls behind Wink's ear, and then started counting the freckles on her right arm, the one holding the book. I did it quietly, so I could still hear her voice. I pressed each freckle with the tip of my finger, and got to twenty-three before my eyes drifted shut.

Wink turned the page and my eyes drifted open again.

Shut.

Open.

And then I saw her.

There, at the top of the ladder.

Poppy.

She was silhouetted against the stars, pale blond hair, light flowing right through her like she was lit from within.

I closed my eyes.

Opened them.

And she was gone.

I'd imagined it.

Hadn't I?

Like the smell of jasmine in my bedroom, I'd imagined it.

Wink closed the book, put it in her pocket, and looked at me. "Midnight, you're shaking. Are you cold?"

I just nodded.

"We should all have some golden milk," she said, louder. "Who wants some golden milk before bed?"

They all wanted it. Even Bee Lee woke up and whispered, "*I* want golden milk."

We all went into the Bell kitchen and drank warm milk with brown sugar and cardamom and turmeric. Mim was out "gathering herbs in the forest by moonlight," Wink told me, casually, like this was normal.

Felix came in, alone, after a while. He poured himself a mug of the steaming yellow milk, leaned against the counter in a contented way, and smiled at his sister. "I'm thinking of taking Charlotte to the Gold Apple Mine tomorrow, to see the horses. She told me she likes horses."

Wink shook her head. "It's a bad time to go to the mine."

Felix raised his eyebrows. "Why?"

Wink took a sip from her cup, and the steam made her face looked flushed. "This week is the anniversary of the accident that killed twenty-seven Gold Apple prospectors and shut down the mine. Their spirits will be active, Felix. You shouldn't go there. Charlotte won't like it. She won't understand it."

Felix nodded at Wink, like this made perfect sense. "Maybe

we'll go in September. The leaves will be really pretty, when they turn."

"I saw something in the woods last night," Peach said, out of nowhere, like kids do. She had a saffron stain around her lips, and her expression was sparkly and impish.

"Was it the white deer? Is he back again?" Wink glanced at me. "There's an albino stag that lives in the forest. We see him sometimes. He's very shy, and very grand."

Bee Lee took my hand and raised her brown eyes to mine. "Greta tells her brothers in *Lost Inside the Emerald Forest* that seeing a white deer is lucky, and that you can wish on one, like a falling star."

Wink smiled at her little sister. "Bee's hoping to wish on our white deer—she wants a ship."

"A big one," Bee said, voice cute and breathless. "With a big wooden wheel and topsails and a captain's log and a telescope."

Wink laughed. "There's no ocean for miles and miles, but Bee's not letting that stop her."

"Good for you, Bee," I said. "Wishes and reality don't mix anyway—"

"No. *No, no, no.*" Peach was shaking her head, her red hair bouncing. Her curls were even messier than Wink's, and longer. The red ringlets dripped down past her elbows. She wore a blue dress and her feet were bare, and very dirty. "It wasn't the white deer I saw. It was a girl."

"We saw her too," Hops said.

"She wore a dark dress," Moon added. "And her hair was the color of stars."

Wink blinked, and her face didn't give anything away, not anything. "When was this? When did you see this girl?"

"Last night, after dinner. We were in the trees, playing Follow the Screams." Peach leaned toward Wink, and put her mouth near her ear, and whispered loud enough for all of us to hear. "She saw me. She didn't see Hops and Moon, because it was their turn to hide, but she saw me and told me she was a ghost and then asked me if I was scared. But I wasn't. Ghosts don't scare me."

"That's true," Wink said, echoing Peach's whisper-yell. "You're not scared of anything."

Peach nodded. "And then I shut my eyes and counted to ten, like you're supposed to whenever you see a ghost or a fairy, and when I opened them she was gone."

Hops yawned and rubbed his freckled nose with his palm. "It wasn't just any girl, in the woods."

Moon yawned too, and stretched his skinny arms over his shaggy red head. "We recognized her. It was that kissing friend of Leaf's. She used to come to the hayloft sometimes."

I stayed calm. I was so calm. I sat there at the kitchen table and just smiled and no way in hell would the kids have guessed that my heart had started screaming.

# Poppy

THREE OF WINK's Orphans were playing in the woods, running between the trees in the dark. The girl would scream, very soft and believable, and the boys would follow.

The girl caught me. She snuck up fast and quiet. I told her I was a ghost. But she only shrugged, and looked like her older sister. I told her she should be scared, that she should run away. I told her I'd come to a bad end. I told her I was wicked to the core, and there was no hope for me now . . . but she just shook her head and went back to her screams.

I watched them, I watched them all later in the hayloft, I climbed the ladder and didn't make a sound, not one sound. I watched Midnight count Wink's freckles. I listened to her go on and on about *The Thing in the Deep*, she never shut up about that book, good god, but Midnight just ate it up, right up, he pushed her big ruby hair behind her ear and looked at her like Leaf never looked at me.

I was doing a lot of thinking lately, there was something about the dark, and the silence, and the being alone, it calmed me down and made me smarter. I was already smart, god knows I was smarter than all of them, but I was smart in a different way now, I took everything in and noticed it, really noticed it. When I stepped into the river I reveled in the cold, I savored the feel of the smooth rocks under my feet. I stopped thinking of myself. I barely thought of myself at all. I thought of myself so little that I began to worry that I'd been the only thing keeping myself in existence . . . and now that I wasn't the center of my attention I'd disappear, poof into thin air, and no one would ever know.

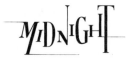

## MIDNIGHT

WINK AND I went to the Blue Twist River, after the Orphans were tucked into their beds.

The moon was bright and blazing, and Wink showed me a shortcut. Down the gravel road between our houses, half a mile, then a quick turn to the left through the nearby cornfield. It was painted mountain corn, the only kind that would grow in our altitude.

The field belonged to a young, bearded organic farmer and Wink said he was always growing strange, new things like yellow beets and purple cauliflower and sweet chocolate peppers and watermelon radishes. The high-end restaurants in Broken Bridge loved it. They bragged about it on chalk sidewalk boards outside their restaurants, *house-made capellini with organic farm leeks, chili flake and Parmesan* or *Colorado red quinoa with grilled white asparagus, pickled mushrooms, Romesco and parsley.* The movie stars came to the mountains to romp in the snow and get away from Hollywood, but that didn't mean they wanted to give up their expensive Los Angeles food.

I followed Wink, the cornstalks clutching at her hair and the hem of her acorn skirt with their grasping paws. The corn was only waist high, but it was already creepy as hell, rustling, rustling in the dark. I breathed a sigh of relief when we pushed through the last bunch of stalks and stepped out onto the bank near the river.

The Blue Twist was clean and cold and ran right down from the mountains, sparkling, churning, melted snow. We sat down on the grass by the edge, Wink across from me. I could no longer hear the rustling of the corn. It was drowned out by the sound of water rushing over stones, and I was glad for it.

"Don't show the Orphans this shortcut, okay, Midnight? Mim thinks they'll drown. I only go here when they're asleep."

I nodded.

Wink slipped off her red sandals and put one foot in the river.

She had small feet. They practically fit in my palm.

She reached into her pocket and took out a candle. She set it on a nearby stone, took out a matchbook, lit the wick.

She reached in again and took out a pack of yellow tarot cards.

A coyote howled, high and eerie. It wasn't too close, but it wasn't that far away either.

Wink shuffled the cards. They were newer than her mother's. Less worn on the corners.

I stared at her as she shuffled.

*We have to talk about it.*

*We have to talk about the letter that Thomas showed me. We have to talk about the fact that Poppy's missing.*

*We have to talk about the girl the Orphans saw in the woods.*

"I'm not nearly as good as Mim or Leaf," Wink said, and her words rushed fast, like they were racing against the river. "I'm much better with auras and ghosts. But Mim won't read cards for me anymore. She read Bee Lee's tarot once and the cards told her Bee would die young. Mim refused to read for us after that. She'll only do our tea leaves and our palms—and even then she only reads for small things."

Wink, red hair falling over her shoulders, laid the cards down in a cross-shaped pattern on the grass.

"Wink?"

"Yes?"

173

"Poppy's missing."

"I know. That's why I'm trying to read the cards."

"That must have been who Peach saw, in the woods, right?"

Wink didn't look at me, didn't say anything.

"What was she doing in the woods?"

Wink shrugged.

"I saw Thomas today, at her house. He showed me a letter, and he said we need to find her . . . that it was a clue to finding her."

Wink looked up. "What did the letter say?"

"She talked about climbing Three Death Jack with Thomas, and being a Greek god, and she said something about jumping, and how Thomas should trust me. What do you make of that, Wink?"

Wink shifted and reached into the pocket of her acorn skirt again. She pulled out a black piece of paper and handed it to me.

I held it next to the candle flame and read.

"It's another clue." Wink's head was down, staring at the cards again, nothing but red curls. "I saw Briggs in the woods today, digging. He's looking for the gold marble, the one in the letter." She paused. "Poppy mentioned you in both of the notes. That's interesting."

It was.

I let a minute or two pass. Rushing river, coyote howling, heart beating.

"What are the cards telling you? Do you know where she is?"

Wink didn't answer.

The candle flickered.

I squinted in the dark and looked at the cards. I saw swords and a wheel. I saw a chalice and a hanged man. I saw a queen of hearts, upside down. I saw a tower.

Wink was quiet for a long time. Finally, finally, she looked up, looked right at me, and frowned. "The cards contradict one another."

A breeze blew up off the river and the candle went out. Darkness.

"Mim is much better at this. I don't have the gift, Midnight. I can't tell where she is." Wink held her finger on one of the cards. "She seems to be in two places at once."

"Why don't we go home and ask Mim to find Poppy? Maybe she'll know what the cards mean."

Wink shook her head. "I already tried that. Mim read Poppy's cards and then wouldn't tell me what they said. She does that sometimes."

Wink reached into her pocket, got a match, and lit the candle again. Her pale face floated back into view. She picked up the cards, put them away, and then wrapped her arms around my neck and pressed her small, cold feet into mine.

"Who did the Orphans see? Who do you think it was, Wink?"

She shrugged again, her shoulders moving against my chest. "Maybe it was Poppy. And maybe they're lying. You never can tell, with Peach and the twins."

I put my arm around Wink's legs and kissed her skinny knees. Wink put her hands in my hair, her thumbs behind my ears. I kissed the skeleton key I found on a chain around her neck. I moved the key with my nose and kissed her collarbone.

"Midnight, what are you afraid of?"

"Hmm?"

"Are you afraid of anything, like how Poppy is afraid of the Roman Luck house?"

"I don't know. Falling, maybe."

"Falling?"

"Falling. I have nightmares about it sometimes."

"Lots of people have nightmares about falling."

"They do?"

"Bee Lee wakes up screaming sometimes. She dreams that she's fallen asleep on a cloud, but then a storm comes up quick and the thunder shakes her off and she falls."

I nodded. "I dream that I'm running through a forest, or a field, and I don't know why. I'm just running from something, and suddenly there's a cliff in front of me, and I don't see it, and then I'm falling down a deep ravine, down past walls of rock and stone, and then my body is breaking, and I can hear the bones all snapping, right before I wake up."

Wink sighed softly. "Mim thinks dreams can foretell the future. But I don't know. I think dreams are just dreams, mostly."

"Well, I think my dream is trying to tell me to stop being a coward. Alabama isn't afraid of heights. He isn't afraid of anything. Not heights, not cliff-jumping, not dying."

"Everyone is afraid of dying, Midnight."

And she didn't say it, and I didn't say it, but we were both thinking of Poppy, tied up in the Roman Luck house, crying, screaming, scared out of her mind, knocking at death's door.

"MIDNIGHT."

My dad, calling down from the attic. I went up the narrow stairs, slow.

He was sitting at his desk, surrounded by books, like always. He looked kind of sleepy.

"Is everything all right?"

"Yeah, Dad. Of course it is."

He took off his thick glasses and rubbed his eyes. He moved his hands away and looked at me again. His light blue irises looked naked without the specs.

"You seem different, Midnight. I know the sound of your step like I know the feel of my own heartbeat. It's heavier this week. And I haven't seen you wear that expression since your . . . since last winter. What's wrong?"

I considered it. Telling him everything. But he wouldn't know what to do about Poppy. He wouldn't know what to do at all. I understood this, suddenly, loudly, like someone had shouted it from a rooftop.

It was something Alabama had always known about him, I think.

"It's all right," I said. I forced a smile and made sure it hit my eyes. "Just girl trouble, Dad. No big deal."

He nodded and put his glasses on. His shoulders relaxed a little. I wondered if he'd been worried I would ask about Mom. About how long she was staying in France.

My dad went back to his books. I went downstairs, to the old black rotary phone in the kitchen. The white tiles felt good under my feet. Cool. The number was on the fridge. I called and it rang and rang. No one picked up. What time was it in France? I didn't know.

I went back upstairs, unbuttoned my shirt, slid off my pants, and climbed into bed. I sunk my face into my pillow, right next to *Will and the Black Caravans*. I breathed in deep. I smelled books, and jasmine.

# WINK

THE CARDS TOLD the whole story, laid out on the grass in swords, wands, cups, coins, queens, kings, knights, and fools. Midnight couldn't read them, but I could, despite what I'd said.

Peach and the twins saw a girl in the woods, but Bee Lee saw something too.

She was down by the Blue Twist a few days ago. She wasn't allowed to go to the river on her own, but she loved to watch the fish in the swirling white water and wouldn't listen to me, not about this.

She came running back down the gravel road, cheeks pink and hair sweaty and sticking to her forehead.

"I saw a girl," she said, "a girl with long yellow hair and a black dress, like a princess in a story. She jumped into the Blue Twist. And you can't swim in the Blue Twist, it goes too fast and you drown. You swallow water and your lungs fill up and you *drown*."

"Show me," I said.

I followed her to the spot, a mile away, down the gravel road . . . but there was no trace of a girl in the water. It was just spinning white curls of river.

"I saw her," Bee said. "I really did, Wink."

I nodded, because I knew.

That was the first time I felt doubt. Just a twinge, just a little bite, nothing more than the Imps and Plum Babies pinching the Hix Sisters in the bluebell field in *The Green Witch of Black Dog Hill*.

That night, after Midnight left, and after I'd run my errand, I snuck in through the kitchen, carefully closing the screen door so it wouldn't slam. I set the basket on the counter and tiptoed upstairs. Bee Lee was sleeping in my bed. She did that when she had nightmares. I crawled in next to her and brushed her hair off her cheek. Her eyes opened.

"Where you been, Wink?"

"Gathering wild strawberries in the forest," I said. "Wild strawberries picked by the light of the moon have magical powers. I'll give you some tomorrow, with sugar and cream. And then we'll see what happens."

"Will I turn into a frog?" she asked.

I nodded.

"Will I turn into a princess?"

I nodded.

She smiled, and closed her eyes again.

# MIDNIGHT

"THERE ARE TWO girls waiting on the front steps for you."

Dad had just gotten back from his run. Three miles every morning, two every night. Sweat trickled down the back of his neck and his whole face was flushed. "Not the blonde and not the redhead. Two new girls."

I pushed back the bowl of homemade granola and milk I was nibbling on. I wasn't hungry anyway. I walked across the kitchen and opened the front screen door.

Stripes.

They turned their heads and looked at me over their shoulders.

"Did you know," Buttercup said, eyes hooded, voice crisp, black hair dripping down, "that Poppy is missing?"

"Missing," Zoe said, echo, echo. Her chin moved up and down and her short brown curls followed.

The morning air had a misty quality, hazy and kind of marvelous. It must have rained again in the night. I looked over at the Bell farm. It was unusually quiet. There was a strange car in the driveway, so Mim was doing a reading. But I didn't see Wink or the Orphans.

Buttercup and Zoe without Poppy and without the rest of the Yellows . . . they seemed less scary, somehow. Almost vulnerable. I sat down on the step next to Zoe and she moved the skirt of her black dress to make room.

I nodded at each of them in turn. "Buttercup. Zoe." It felt strange to say their names for the very first time without the usual feeling of dread hitting my tongue. "Yeah, I know Poppy is missing. Why are you here?"

"I don't know," Buttercup said, and her black eyes reminded me of Wink's, suddenly. Open and innocent. "I mean, yes I do."

"Yes, we do," said Zoe.

Buttercup slipped the skull-shaped backpack off her shoulder and rummaged around inside. She pulled out something thin and black, and held it between her fingertips, gingerly, like it was poison.

"Take it."

I did. It was a small sheet of lined paper, folded in half. I just looked at it, sitting on my palm.

"Poppy likes to write on black paper with a silver pen," Buttercup said. "I found it in my backpack this morning."

I opened it. Silver letters on a charcoal background.

It was Poppy's handwriting, just like Thomas's letter. And Briggs's. I knew the loop of her *g*. I recognized the plump belly of her *b*. It was as familiar to me as the blue veins in her lily-white arms.

*Buttercup and Zoe,*

*It's for the best, I swear it is, and I'm always right, I always am.*

*Do you remember that time we went apple picking last fall? We stole a bucket of them from that big old tree near the abandoned elementary school and I had you both write down apple poems as I made them up on the spot, and the poems were all about me, about how I was gray-eyed and apple-cheeked, about how I ruled with an iron fist and how I was the apple of everyone's eye.*

*How could you stand me?*
*I can't even stand myself, not anymore.*
*You should go talk to Midnight.*
*He has things to tell you.*

"I have a bad feeling," Buttercup said, and shuddered, quick and gentle like the shimmering leaves of the nearby aspen tree. She rubbed her long, thin fingers up and down over her striped-stocking legs. Her fingernails weren't painted black, like usual. They were just a plain, natural pink. "I think Poppy did something to herself."

183

Zoe just nodded.

That feeling came back, the one from the Roman Luck house, flu sick and too little sleep and clammy-skinned fear. "She wouldn't. Poppy's not that kind of girl."

"Who knows what kind of girl Poppy is." Zoe this time, all on her own.

"What things do you have to tell us?" Buttercup asked. "She said you had things to tell us, in the letter."

Poppy wanted me to tell them about the Roman Luck house. About what me and Wink did to her there. I knew she did.

But instead I just shrugged, quick, like Wink. "Poppy wrote notes on black paper to Thomas and Briggs too . . . maybe this is what she wanted you to know. Thomas thinks they're clues to finding out where she's gone. I haven't made up my mind, though. I'm still thinking."

Buttercup gave me a small smile then, no red lipstick. "We've decided that we're sorry we were mean to you in the past, Midnight."

I stared at her for a second. She seemed sincere. "It's okay."

"It's not okay." Zoe. The thick stubs of her brown curly hair rubbed against her cheekbones. She was looking down at her black boots, toes touching, ankles out. "Poppy was a bad influence on us. We can see that now."

Buttercup nodded.

I thought of Poppy, in the Roman Luck house, her arms

above her head, dried blood on her face, whispering *you didn't come back, you left me here and didn't come back. . . .*

If Poppy was a bad influence, then so was I.

Everything went hazy at the edges suddenly, blurry, blurrrrrr . . .

I blinked. And breathed in deep. Again, and again.

"I'll walk you girls home," I said.

WE FOUND BRIGGS and Thomas on our way back into town. They were half a mile from the Roman Luck place. Briggs was standing in the middle of three small mounds of dirt, a shovel nearby on the ground. He looked up at us and wiped his hand across his forehead. His fingernails were dirty, and black creases stretched across the skin of his palms.

Thomas stood next to him, close, like they'd just been talking.

"What are you two doing?" Buttercup had her arms crossed over her chest, and her elbows were moving up and down with her breath.

Briggs whispered something, cleared his throat, spoke louder. "I'm looking for a marble." Pause. "It's stupid, I know. I'll never find it. Still . . . I had to try. You're supposed to be helping me look, by the way." Briggs glanced at me out the corner of his eyes.

I looked right back at him. "I saw your letter. Wink showed me."

Thomas reached into the zippered pocket on his designer jeans and took out his own black piece of Poppy paper. "I was just telling Briggs that I think the letters are clues."

"Clues to finding Poppy," Buttercup added.

"Why the hell would she run off in the first place?" Briggs groaned, deep and kind of sad. He yanked off his sweaty T-shirt and threw it on the ground. "What happened to spark all this?"

I picked up the shovel and put it behind my back.

I had to tell them. I had to suck it up and be the hero and tell the Yellows what happened to their fearless leader.

"Wink and I tricked her. We tied her to the grand piano in the Roman Luck house and left her there all night."

All four Yellows went still.

"You did *what*?" Briggs. His head cocked to the side.

My palms were sweaty on the wooden handle, sweaty and slick. "We tied her to the grand piano and left her in the music room until dawn. When we got back she was . . . she was *dimmed*, if that makes sense. I never thought . . . I never thought it would crush her, not like that. And I haven't seen her since that morning."

Which was a lie, because I *had* seen her, on the top of the hayloft, just for a split second.

And I'd smelled her perfume in my room every night too.

But the Yellows didn't need to know this. I might have imagined it all anyway.

I focused on Briggs, since he was the one I was the most worried about. His face was flushed, down his cheekbones, across his neck.

This was it. The Yellows were going to beat the hell out of me. And I had it coming.

Briggs grabbed for the shovel and it slid right out of my sweaty palms. I didn't even resist. He put his arm back and . . .

And threw it. Right past me. It hit one of the trees, hard, and fell to the ground, a quiet, gentle thud.

After that Briggs just stood there, staring at me.

He didn't look angry anymore. He just looked tired.

"We don't blame you, for tricking her." Buttercup put her hand on my forearm and rubbed her fingers up and down, from my wrist to my elbow. "What Poppy did to Wink at the Roman Luck party was unforgivable."

"We helped Poppy do it." The wind picked up and blew Thomas's shaggy blond hair all around his head, like it was trying to get his attention. "We helped her humiliate Wink."

Briggs kept staring at me, one blue eye, one green. "I saw someone out here in the woods last night. A girl that looked just like Poppy. I only saw her for a second, right before she disappeared back into the dark. You want to know what I think?"

No one nodded, but he went on anyway.

"I think Poppy is fucking with us."

Long pause.

"Or she's dead, and she's haunting us." Thomas said it kind of defiantly, chin up, like he expected us to start laughing.

Which Briggs did. "So she's writing letters *from beyond the grave?* That's so stupid. Poppy is a fighter, like me. She's not a quitter."

"Poppy is a lot of things," I said. And meant it. "Look, Wink and I started this. Whatever happened in the Roman Luck house, whatever Poppy went through, it led to her going missing. I'm to blame."

Buttercup turned suddenly and gave me a hug. Her arms were long and warm.

My mom had always said that fear brought out the truth in people. She based entire books on it. I guess Buttercup's truth was better than I'd thought.

"I'm worried about Poppy," she whispered in my ear. "I'm scared for her."

"Me too," I said.

"I'm going home." Thomas started walking away, talking to us over his shoulder. "I'm going to study my letter and then I'm going to search every damn nook and cranny until I find her."

"We'll help you," Buttercup said. And Zoe nodded. And Briggs followed behind.

# POPPY

THE THING ABOUT Briggs, the secret thing, was that he'd never hurt a fly. He was a bully, and like most bullies, like all bullies but me, he was a baby underneath it all. At least Midnight was a baby straight up, there was something to respect in that, there was. I said before that Thomas was the sad one, the sensitive one, but Briggs . . . I'd once seen Briggs cry over a spotted owl in the park that had broken its wing and kept hopping around because he couldn't fly. Briggs tried to hide his tears but I saw them, and heard the way he was sniffling too, on his knees in the grass, and his voice was thick and choked and he kept asking me over and over what he should do, as if I was some sort of spotted owl wing-healer.

And right before the bird, Briggs had been taunting a nerdy little kid about his thick glasses and the soccer ball he couldn't kick worth a damn, and the whole time it never occurred to him, the contradiction.

I used to meet the Yellows in the morning, not too early, at Lone Tree Joe. In the summer it was filled with wealthy, weasel-faced hipsters on break from school and staying in their parents' vacation homes until September, but I was

Poppy and had to have the best even if it meant rubbing elbows with the non-local trust-fund brat packs.

It seems like a million years ago, getting expensive lattes, shaken with ice, just the right combination of espresso to milk, just the right toffee color or I'd complain.

I once convinced Buttercup and Zoe to help me dig my own grave. We were bored and I was in a macabre mood and I wanted to see what it was like, to lie in the dirt six feet under like a dead person. We tromped out to the woods with shovels stolen from outside Loren's Hardware store. They whined and whined but eventually we got a good trench dug out between two trees. I plopped down inside and crossed my arms over my chest like Wednesday Addams, and Zoe leaned over the edge and said something about worms and spiders, but I didn't care, I stayed there for twenty minutes with my eyes closed. I wasn't scared, it didn't even feel that morbid, it just felt sort of peaceful, really.

Briggs caught me watching him in the woods.

He called out my name, kind of sad and desperate, but by then I was already gone, flitting through the night like one of Wink's fairies.

Briggs had been digging in the dirt and muttering about a *golden marble* like some half-crazed, sweating farm laborer, and I couldn't figure out why, not for a while. I had to sink down and lie on the dirt in the forest and put some pieces together before I got to the bottom of it.

# WINK

I saw Buttercup and Zoe on Midnight's steps.

Buttercup, sleek as a selkie, smooth black hair and olive skin like the taciturn enchantress in *Lost Lies and Runaway Sighs.*

Zoe, sparkly hazel eyes and thick black lashes and a small, pointed nose like the fay in *Rat Hall and the Broom Girls.* When she smiled at Midnight, her smile was as sparkly as her eyes.

All three talked for a while and then walked right through my farm, right into the forest, and down the path.

I got the Orphans out of bed and took them into town to get ice cream for breakfast. I did this sometimes in the summer, when Mim had her readings. We went to the little place by the library that was run by a witchie lady with long white hair. She opened the shop at ten in the morning because she believed that ice cream was sometimes for breakfast too. Bee Lee got strawberry, she always got strawberry, but you never could tell about Peach and the twins. Felix went for the pistachio, and so did I.

We were all sitting on the green benches in the park, eating in the sun, when I saw her, standing in a brick alley across the road, the shadows surrounding her like a pack of wolves.

No one else could see her. I knew they couldn't. Just me.

I gave the rest of my waffle cone to Hops and walked across the street without another thought, like she was the blond, bloodthirsty siren in *Three Songs for a Drowning*.

I walked into the alley, bravely, right into the pack of wolf-shadows . . . but she was already gone.

# MIDNIGHT

I STOOD IN the kitchen and listened. Dad was upstairs in his attic, on the phone. His voice drifted down through the cracks in the floorboards and settled on my ears like dust. He was speaking German with the occasional Latin phrase thrown in. I only spoke a bit of French, but Alabama was fluent in it, like our mom. My dad spoke four languages, if you counted Latin, which I did.

His voice was a song I didn't want to end. It made me feel safe. It made me feel . . . normal.

There was a knock on the front door. I'd been expecting it, somehow.

Peach was standing on the steps, red curls and bare feet.

"Follow me," she said.

So I followed her, short strong legs pounding into the ground with focused, kid-like purpose. Across the road and into the garden. Wink was sitting in the strawberry patch, feet in the dirt, fat white clouds shielding her from the passionate noonday sun.

"I was up in the hayloft," Peach said to both me and Wink, now that she'd gathered us together. "It didn't smell like hay. It smelled like tea, or flowers. And this was on the floor."

She handed me a piece of black paper.

Wink watched me take it, face calm and passive, like it was nothing, just an ordinary thing, another note from a missing girl, left in a hayloft.

I felt Peach staring at me. "I can read," she said. "I can read all kinds of things. I'm really good at it, better than you, probably." I hadn't questioned her reading skills, it hadn't even occurred to me, but Peach wasn't the kind of kid to let that stop her from putting me in my place.

I didn't want to open the letter.

I wouldn't.

I had to.

I did.

My fingers were clammy. They left damp smudges on the page.

*Midnight.*

*It's up to you.*

*Show me what you're made of.*

*Gather the Yellows.*

*Go to the woods.*

*Find me.*

*Find me in the mist.*

I read it again. And again. And then I gave the note to Wink.

Peach shook her curly hair, chin to the right and left. "I read the note and that's how I knew it wasn't for any of us Orphans. *Going into the mist* is what Mim calls contacting the spirits. If you're having a séance, I want to come."

"No," Wink said, softly. "Not to this. But later we can hold another séance in the hayloft, just us, and I'll let you be the medium this time, all right?"

Peach tapped her finger on the tip of her nose and started nodding. "I'll make a great medium. The best ever."

Wink smiled, and the tips of her ears popped out between piles of red hair. "You will," she replied, very serious.

Peach ran off, shouting to Hops and Moon, wherever they were, about how they were going to be so jealous because Wink put her in charge of a séance and soon she would be bossing ghosts and spirits around, just wait until tomorrow in the hayloft.

Wink picked the last three ripe strawberries off their green stems, and gave one to me.

I fiddled with the strawberry, spinning it in my palm. "The flowery smell in the hayloft that Peach was talking about? It's jasmine."

"Poppy wore jasmine oil." Wink looked up, green eyes wide open and innocent, like always.

I nodded. I didn't tell her about my bedroom, about how the sheets and pillows smelled like Poppy at night. I just couldn't do it. It came too close to admitting that Poppy had been in my bed. And I didn't want Wink to know this.

"Buttercup and Zoe came to my house this morning. Buttercup found a black note from Poppy too."

"What did it say?" Wink ate a strawberry, two small bites.

"Something about me and something about the time they went apple picking. I walked them home and we found Briggs and Thomas in the woods. I told them, Wink. I told them we're the reason Poppy is missing. I told them that we tied her up and left her in the Roman Luck house."

Wink dug her small, pink toes into the black soil, past her heel, up to the ankle. "I think Poppy threw herself in the Blue Twist, Midnight. I think she drowned. And I think one of the Yellows is writing the notes."

The world started spinning. I dropped my strawberry and pressed my hands to my eyes. *Stop with the blur, stop all the blurring, I can't take it, I can't . . .*

I sat down in the dirt and Wink's arms went around me, tight. I took deep breaths and moved my hands away from my face so I could hug her back. She was wearing a fraying green cardigan over her overalls and she smelled liked strawberries and soil and jasmine.

# PoPPy

I WAS THERE when Midnight found the Yellows down by the river, waiting for my body to wash ashore or something, though it never would, it never, ever would.

I watched them all and they didn't see me, not one damn speck of me. I liked being invisible, I was learning things, there were so many things I'd missed before, back when I always needed to be the center of attention.

Midnight told them all about some letter I supposedly wrote that said I wanted them to come together in the woods for a séance, as if I would ever ever ever ask them to hold a séance and contact my spirit, everyone knows that I don't believe in that crap, Grandpa never had any patience for the mystical and neither do I. That stuff was for Wink and her mother and all their other fairy ilk, not for me.

Midnight got three of them to agree right off the bat. Thomas wanted to get out his Ouija board and ask it about the letter clues, and Buttercup and Zoe nodded in that twee twin way that used to drive me up a wall. Briggs just laughed, though, he knelt down and splashed cold river water on his face and just laughed, and went on and on about how I hadn't even been missing that many days, and I'd gone missing before, and it was nothing to get worked up about, the bastard. Midnight reminded him what he'd been up to lately, digging around in the forest for a marble like a lunatic, all because he'd gotten a letter too, and Briggs shut up after that.

I was there when they met in a little meadow near the Roman Luck house at midnight, flashlights dancing across the forest floor. I was watching. Thomas set up the Ouija board on the ground, right on the pine needles and dirt. He was so serious and careful and solemn about it that I half wanted to laugh and half wanted to put my hand on my heart and swear him my everlasting loyalty.

They set their fingers on the pointer and then started asking so many questions that the Ouija board could never have kept up, even if it actually worked, which it didn't. Thomas asked about Three Death Jack and the Greek gods and what it all meant and I remembered the time the two of us sat up on the mountain watching the skiers and it made me kind of sad and nostalgic. Briggs asked about the gold marble and tea-cups and lemonade and it sounded like *Alice in Wonderland* gibberish, except it wasn't.

Buttercup and Zoe asked about apple picking and apple poems, and Midnight asked if the mist was a spiritual place or a real place and the pointer never moved, not once. Not even a flicker. Finally, finally, Midnight said they needed Wink, Wink could find me, if anyone could, and that was when it all really began, when it got aching and beautiful and palpable and true. They all started fighting, quiet at first, and then louder and louder until their voices echoed through the trees like the black-haired Bloodly Boys at one of their midnight feasts . . . oh hell, I was talking like her now, like Wink.

Anyway, anyway, you should have heard them, arguing about who knew me best, and why I really disappeared, why I would run away, why I would throw myself in the Twist. Thomas said I did it because I was sad, but that's because he's sad, and Briggs said I would never do it, because I'm a fighter, but that's because he's a fighter, and Buttercup said I felt guilty about all my past cruelty because she feels guilty about hers, and Zoe said that if I wanted to run away or throw myself in the river it was my right to do so, because she wants that to be her right too.

And none of them, not one, came close to the truth.

Except Midnight.

He repeated what he'd said earlier, about how they needed Wink, and off they went to get her.

THEY NEEDED MY help. I knew they would.

I washed my hair with cinnamon soap and put on my acorn skirt and waited for them in the hayloft.

I told them we had to have the séance in the Roman Luck house. That it all had to end where it began. I took one of the extra quilts Mim kept in a trunk at the top of the stairs and I threw it over my shoulder and then grabbed my basket and we walked through the woods together.

I laid the blanket on the floor in the music room. I took three white candles out of my basket and placed them in the middle. I knew how it went. I'd seen Mim hold séances seven times. She didn't do it for every client, only the special ones, the special ones with a lot of money. I went off to the corner and stood there silently for a bit, as if I was preparing myself, but it was mainly for dramatic effect.

Midnight was quiet, and didn't say much. He was scared.

All good Heroes are scared, if they know the evil they face.

Briggs asked why I didn't bring a Ouija board and when I told him I didn't have one he looked like he didn't believe me.

Thomas clung to the shadows in the corner of the room like he was trying to hide, like he was Anthony Twilight in *Fourteen Stolen Things*.

Buttercup and Zoe cuddled into each other and whispered in each other's ears and held hands.

I lit the candles.

It began.

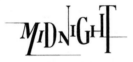

## MIDNIGHT

ME AND THE Yellows found Wink in the hayloft.

Her eyes had a look in them when she saw us all climbing up the ladder, like she'd known we'd come for her.

She grabbed the quilt and basket that she'd already packed, that's how ready she was. Wink and I walked side by side down the path, not talking, like that very first time, when we'd stumbled into Poppy's party.

Wink set the unlit candles on the blanket and then stood in one of the corners, in the dark. I figured she was meditating, or whatever it is that mediums do. I sat on the green sofa and listened to the floorboards groaning in the hallway, though no one was walking on them. I listened to the tree branches scraping the un-smashed pieces of the bay window. I listened to the old house make its old house sounds, rasp, creak, groan.

Here I was again, in the Roman Luck house in the middle of the night.

Tricking Wink and then tricking Poppy and kissing them both and tying them both up . . . and now I was back in the house again and Poppy was missing and I'd gathered the Yellows for a séance.

Briggs tried to make a few jokes, about how stupid séances are, and how it's all bullshit, just rapping tables and sliding panels and fake beards, but no one laughed or even looked at him.

We all sat down on the blanket in a circle.

Wink lit the candles.

I MADE EVERYONE hold hands. I looked very grave and said that if they let go during the séance bad things would happen. Which wasn't true, I just wanted to see if they believed me, and they did.

Midnight was on my right, his fingers strong and sturdy,

like Thief's. Thomas was on my left. He had long, elfish fingers that were warm, almost hot. I waited until Buttercup and Briggs and Zoe were clasped and ready.

Nothing happened.

I asked Poppy if she was present.

Nothing happened.

The house creaked and moaned and the Yellows breathed and twitched and fidgeted and Midnight squeezed my hand.

Nothing happened.

I called out to Poppy again. I told her I was ready and listening.

Nothing happened.

The candles flickered and the wind picked up outside, but I wasn't cold. I was warm suddenly, warm like I had a fire burning in me. I held my breath and pictured myself as a cavern, deep and open, a vessel that needed to be filled, just as Mim had taught me.

Nothing happened.

a

n

d

t

h

e

n

My head flipped back. My mouth opened and my eyes shut and my tongue fluttered and the words . . . poured . . .

I thrashed and whispered and shouted and the words *poured and poured.*

*I was Autumn Lind with the kitchen knife, and then I was Martin, screaming and screaming, the blood gushing out, gushing right here in this room, tell my children I love them, tell them, tell them, and then I was Autumn again, choking and shaking as my neck snapped in the noose . . .*

I thrashed and screamed and then the words . . .

s

t

o

p

p

e

d.

I brought my head upright again, opened my eyes, relaxed my shoulders. Midnight and the Yellows were shaking and I could feel their fear in the air, crackling like static during a thunderstorm.

And right on cue, it started raining outside, like I'd commanded it, like I'd called it down from the night sky, the rain tore at the broken window and splashed inside and hit me on the cheek and I was the Queen now, bow down before me, this is how it was meant to be, this was how it was supposed to be, all of them watching and waiting on my every word, breaths held . . .

I yanked my hands free from Midnight and Thomas, one swift move, and got to my feet.

"God, you're all such losers," I said, first thing out of my mouth, and they all just stared and stared, as if I hadn't called each of them a loser countless times in the past, hundreds, thousands, millions.

I looked down at myself, touched my hair, stroked my bony knees with my palms. "Can you believe this shit? *Feral Bell.* Beggars can't be choosers, I guess."

They stared and stared and I just let them, let them take me in.

*"Poppy . . . Poppy, where are you? Are you okay? What happened to you?"* Squeaking, pathetic little voices.

"I'm dead," I whispered. And then laughed. "*Dead.* I'm dead and this house is my tomb and I want you to burn it down. *I want you to burn the Roman Luck house to the ground."*

The rain pelted in and the lightning ran slick across the stars and I stood there with my hands on my hips and all of them watching my every move, frozen with fear, their pitiful faces stretched and open and so, so terrified.

They asked me questions, so many questions, who did this and who did that and what about the letters and what about the clues and oh, they were so sorry, so very sorry . . . and it bored me to tears, so finally I put my hands on Thomas's shoulders and straddled him, one skinny leg nestling up to each hip, knees squeezing in. I kissed him, I kissed him deep, I writhed my body and swung my hair and he kissed me back, I wasn't sure he would, but oh yes he did, he pulled his other hand free and put both on me while they all just stared, and then I whispered in his ear, *Remember the night we did it in the rain, in the wet grass by the Blue Twist? The cold drops hit our bare skin and we shivered like ghosts and were slippery like eels . . . I never told anyone, did you?*

And Thomas shook his head and then I got up and went around the circle, I whispered in all their ears, I whispered all their secrets, and they watched and stared and I sashayed around them and let my hips flick side to side, let my long spine arch and my hair swing, I was the Queen, I was the villain, I ruled them all. I let their worship wash right over me like a cool rain, like the rain outside, cooling down the sky, and it felt so good I wanted to scream scream scream with joy, keep staring, you fools, keep staring, soak it up, soak it up, soak me up, like rays of sunshine after a storm, there'll never be anyone like me again, never ever ever ever.

Midnight was last, I went around the circle and saved him for last, I sat in his lap and gripped his hair in my fingers and he looked horrified, beautifully and genuinely horrified and my red hair fell around his cheeks and I pushed my chest into his and whispered in his ear, *I'm sorry I teased you about* the magic tricks that one time, I felt bad about it afterward, I really did, I'm sorry I teased you about everything, Midnight, all of this, the letters and the séance, all of it was for you, just so I could say I miss you, god, how I miss you, time goes slower where I am, it feels like years since I last crawled into your bed, years and years, I just wanted to see you one last time, Midnight, I needed to say I'm sorry, I—

He pushed me off of him, right off, like I burned, like I was poison.

And my foot hit a candle and the candle hit the blanket and then . . .

Fire.

## MIDNIGHT

WINK MADE US all hold hands. I took hers in my right, Buttercup's in my left.

Jasmine. That was first.

The smells of the Roman Luck house, the smells of dust and rot and woods and mold . . . gone, all gone.

And the air filled with jasmine.

The Yellows smelled it too. Their eyes went wide. I saw it. They knew what it meant. The smell was thick, sickly, and I wanted to cover my nose with my hand but Wink had warned us not to let go.

Wink.

"Poppy, are you here?" she said. Her voice was calm and clear and soft.

Silence.

I squeezed her hand.

"I'm listening, Poppy. I'm ready."

Silence.

It started small. Wink's eyes closed, and her lips drew tight, *tight*, as if her face was trying to swallow her mouth. Her cheeks sunk in. Hard, dark, hollow bruises.

The Yellows stopped turning their heads and sniffing the air. We all froze.

Wink's head tilted back, so far her hair touched the floor, and her body went rigid, it *snapped*, like a rope pulled tight, like the rope that we used to tie up Poppy, snap, her wrists to the piano.

The things that came out of her mouth . . .

Gibberish and swearing and moaning. Guttural groans and sobs. On and on. Wink jerked and strained against my fingers but I didn't let go, I didn't let go. Her head whipped sideways *and her back arched and tears streamed from her green eyes . . .*

What should I do? I wanted to stop it, I had to stop it, but I was scared, so scared, was this what Poppy had wanted? For

Wink to come to the Roman Luck house and let the unforgivables in, let them destroy her too? Wink said bad things
would happen if we let go, but I wanted to let go of her hand,
*I wanted to shake her, shake the unforgivables out of her, god, it*
*was horrible, no wonder Poppy had died, left alone with them,*
*how could we have done it?*

Wink started screaming and I screamed with her and Zoe
and Buttercup screamed too and Briggs shouted and Thomas
was silent and . . .

And, suddenly, it stopped.

Wink hushed. Everything, her voice, her arms, her hair,
*hush.*

Her fingers went limp.

She straightened, and opened her eyes.

The thunderstorm hit, right then, right that very second.
Rain slapped the broken shards of the bay window, plop, plop,
and then faster and faster. Thunder cracked so hard the ground
started shaking, or maybe it was just me, shaking and shaking.
I couldn't seem to stop shaking.

Wink yanked her hand away. Her fingers slipped right
through mine. I let out a little groan as it happened. I'd been
so sure that if I just held on to her everything would be okay
in the end.

She stood up. She flipped her red curly hair behind her
shoulders, and put her hands on her tiny hips.

"God, you're all such losers," she said.

And it wasn't Wink's voice, small and whispery and soft. It was arrogant. Sultry.

Wink touched her hair, and looked at her arms, and her legs, smooth and graceful twists, eyebrows raised, lips pressed together in a pout.

"Can you believe this shit? *Feral Bell.* Beggars can't be choosers, I guess."

The chill started in my heart and shuddered through the rest of me. My scalp stung and my skin itched.

I still held Buttercup's hand in my left. I'd forgotten all about it until she was suddenly squeezing my fingers so hard it took my breath away.

*"Poppy . . . Poppy, where are you? Are you okay? What happened to you?"* Thomas had tears coming down his face, fast, like the rain outside.

"I'm dead." And she laughed. And it wasn't Wink's laugh, it didn't remotely sound like Wink's laugh, whispers and chinkling toy piano keys. It was cold and hard and sneering and Poppy, all Poppy.

"*Dead.* I'm dead and this house is my tomb and I want you to burn it down, *I want you to burn the Roman Luck house to the ground.*"

None of us moved, none.

*"Where are you? Can we help you? We're so sorry, we didn't*

*believe it, didn't believe you'd really do it . . ."* Buttercup's voice fluttered, in and out, like the candle flames.

"Wink and Midnight tied me up and left me here, but the unforgivables did their part too. Freckle-faced Feral was right about them." And she laughed again, hollow and mean and cold. "They're here right now, breathing down your necks . . . except you can't even see them, you fools. They won't hurt me anymore, I'm beyond all that, they've got their evil focused on you now."

"Who's here? What are the unforgivables?" Briggs, voice strong and quivering at the same time.

Wink sighed . . .

I mean Poppy . . .

I mean Wink . . .

"This is so *boring*. I'm tired of answering questions. Just shut up, all of you, and let me do what I came here to do."

She climbed on Thomas then, cuddled right up to him, knees on each side of his hips.

She kissed him.

He kissed back.

It was Wink's red hair and Wink's skinny spine, but it was Poppy's lips and Poppy's gestures and it was horrifying. *Horrifying.*

She put her mouth by Thomas's ear and began to whisper and whisper. His eyes filled with tears again and his mouth parted and he looked so sad . . . and so filled with joy . . .

Then she was up and onto the next person.

Zoe.

Buttercup.

Whispers and stricken looks and horrifying, horrifying.

Briggs, she kissed him too, freckled hands on his cheeks. My heart broke watching it. Split in two. And I didn't know if it was because Wink was kissing him, or Poppy, or both.

She sat in my lap last. She grabbed my hair in her fingers and her curls burrowed into my neck and her chest pressed into mine.

And the things she said, *the things she said*, Poppy's voice coming out of Wink's lips. She said she was sorry. She said it over and over.

But Poppy never said she was sorry, not ever.

*Not ever.*

I couldn't stand it. I couldn't stand one more second of it.

I pushed her away from me.

The blanket moved, and her foot knocked over the candle, and then flames, flames and fire.

# WINK

I WAS ME again, and the blanket was on fire, and then the edge of Zoe's dress.

Midnight jumped to his feet and started stomping out the flames and Zoe rolled on the ground and Buttercup screamed.

The fire flew across the floor and up the curtains and over the piano. Thomas and Briggs tore off their shirts and whacked at the burning orange waves, but the smoke just grew and grew, like magic beanstalks up into the sky. I couldn't see, the smoke, tears running down my face. I stumbled, hit the piano stool, hands helped me up, I stumbled again, where was the window? I couldn't see, couldn't see, someone pulled on my arm, and then it was there, the bay window, right in front of me. I pushed through, coughing, coughing, and I fell down onto the dirt, right next to Buttercup. Zoe helped us up, my eyes burned and I blinked and blinked but still couldn't see. I grabbed Zoe's hand and Buttercup grabbed mine and we ran toward the forest.

I smelled pine and knew I'd reached the trees. I let go of the girls' fingers and started rubbing my eyes, streaks of blood across my cheeks, palms cut by the jagged window glass. Buttercup and Zoe scattered in the dark. They didn't wait. They ran like thieves, like the twelve girls in *Between the Dragon and the Wrath,* not even glancing over their shoulders as they disappeared in the dark. Briggs and Thomas ran past me next, scared white faces and panting open mouths.

I looked back, back at the Roman Luck house, the smoke crawling up and up like it was trying to touch the moon, it didn't care about the rain, the storm couldn't touch the fire at all . . .

*Crash.*

The roof caved in.

*Crash, crash, crash.*

I looked around, I wanted to take his hand . . .

But he wasn't there.

Midnight *wasn't there.*

THE SMOKE WAS everywhere, I coughed and coughed, I counted the shapes, one, two, three, four, five, they were all through the window, they were safe, I grabbed the sill, careful of the broken glass . . .

And then I heard it. Thunder.

Except it wasn't thunder, it was the roof.

I saw the crack. The ceiling. I was conscious long enough to see it split in two . . . plaster loosening, falling . . . then dust . . . smoke . . . my lungs . . . dark.


# Poppy

I WAS THERE, watching. I hated hated hated the Roman Luck house, but I was there anyway. I moved with the shadows, and no one saw me. No one ever saw me anymore.

I watched it all, I laughed when Wink laughed and winced when Midnight winced.

Fire.

I was there when the roof caved in. I was there when everyone crawled out of the window, everyone but Midnight. I was there when he hit the floor. I grabbed him, I didn't even think about it, I just grabbed him and pulled him down the hall and out the back door, wooden beams plummeting all around us.

# Midnight

I OPENED MY eyes. Forest floor. Earth and pine needles.

The sun was rising, I could see the light . . .

I turned my head. It wasn't the sun. It was the fire. The Roman Luck fire. Fifty yards away, through the trees. I tried to sit up, but my bones felt so heavy, so damn heavy. My lungs burned. It hurt to breathe.

I smelled jasmine.

Smoke, and jasmine.

And then she was there, face in front of mine, blond hair tickling my throat.

"*Midnight*," she said.

Her voice sounded different. Hollow, and sad.

"*Poppy.*"

I reached up to touch her, fingertips stretching toward her cheek . . .

But my hand hit air.

She was already gone.

I FOUND WINK in the forest. She gave a little cry when she saw me. I put my arms around her. We both reeked of smoke, but it smelled good on her.

"I couldn't find you after we all crawled out the window," Wink whispered into my neck. "What happened, Midnight? *Where did you go?*"

Sirens in the distance, sharp and shrill.

"I passed out from the smoke, just as the roof caved in."

I felt her arms tighten around me, elbows locking in.

"Someone pulled me out the back door, Wink. Into the forest."

"Who?" Soft breath on my neck.

But I didn't answer her.

"DO YOU REMEMBER anything?" I asked, a half hour later in the hayloft. "Do you remember what you did? What happened, before the blanket caught on fire?"

Wink shook her head. "One second I was taking your hand, and the next I woke up to screaming, and flames."

"You don't remember the unforgivables?"

She shook her head again.

Dawn was coming. I could feel it more than see it. The air was snappy and crystal cold, and it smelled good, after all the smoke.

"You were *her*, Wink. Her voice, her gestures, her expressions, everything."

She didn't say anything for a while. We were leaning against a hay bale and her head was on my stomach. I ran my thumb down the inside of her skinny arm and stopped at her wrist, so I could feel her pulse. Tick, tick, tick. She'd cut her palms on the bay window glass, and there were jagged streaks of dried blood running across her hands. I kissed one of the cuts, and she flinched.

"Did you like me being her?" she asked, soft, soft.

"No," I said.

"Are you sure?"

"Yes."

She turned and pulled my shirt up, and kissed my stomach, right above my belly button, her hands on my waist.

"Are you *sure*?"

Her lips on my ribs, across my chest . . .

"Yes, I'm sure."

Her fingernails up my sides, gently, gently . . .

Her red curls, everywhere. . .

And then she sat up and kissed me on the mouth, lips full on mine, deep, deeper. It went on and on.

She slid her left leg over me, squeezed up her knees, right into my hips, one on each side . . .

She flipped her hair and arched her back, just the once, just in the exact right way.

And I knew.

I *knew.*

I pulled away, just as the first stroke of sun hit the hayloft. I pulled away and looked straight at her.

She didn't have to say it. I read it right there in her green sunrise gaze, read it like a page in a book.

"Poppy's not dead," I whispered.

"Of course not," Wink whispered back.

I WENT HOME. I showered and crawled into bed. My pillow still smelled like jasmine.

I got up in a few hours. I made tea for my dad, and brought it to him in the attic.

"You hear the sirens last night?" he asked, nose buried in an ancient copy of *Don Quixote.*

"Yeah. The Roman Luck house burned."

He didn't ask me how I knew. "Must have been the lightning."

"Must have been."

He nodded but didn't look up. He knew I was lying. He didn't say anything, though, didn't grill me or force a confession. And he never would. For better or worse, that was my dad.

I went down to the kitchen and grabbed a map out of the drawer.

The Bell farm was quiet as I walked on by, all the animals

asleep, and the humans too. The farm seemed different. It was still peaceful, and magical . . . but it had a small darkness to it now, like a black cloud on the horizon, like when Thief walks through the Forest of Sighs and hears the far-off howling of the Witch Wolves beneath the singing of the birds and the rustling of the green leaves and the murmuring of the River Red.

I turned and went down the neglected gravel road. Left, then right, then over the hill.

To the Gold Apple Mine.

I WATCHED MIDNIGHT walk down the road, and I knew where he was going.

He didn't see me. I was good at hiding. I'd learned how, from the book *Sneaks and Shadows.*

I taught Poppy how to hide too. She was a quick learner.

The Wolf first came to our door on the arm of my brother Leaf. She liked him for his being so savage and wild. She had that in her too, though mostly it was all buttoned up and locked in like the drugged woman in *Blood Red and White.* The Wolf was younger then. She was still just Poppy. She was still just a girl, like the rest of us. And Leaf could handle Poppy. He knew what he was up against. He didn't have a big, soft heart like Midnight, with all its wide-open windows and doors and easy ways of entering. Leaf's heart had barbed wire and alarms and vicious, barking dogs. He was safe from her teeth.

Outside the hayloft, I was invisible. I was a ghost.

But inside the hayloft, it was different.

The first time Poppy found me up there, reading to the Orphans, she was with Leaf. Later she started coming up there just to find me. She said she wanted to hear my stories. She said she liked the way I read. And the way my hair curled. And the way my freckles reminded her of my brother.

The Wolf called me Feral outside the hayloft, but inside she called me Wink. She taught me how to keep my lips soft when I kissed. She taught me how to stroke skin with my fingertips, until the goose bumps came.

The White Witch gave Edmund Turkish Delight and convinced him to betray his brother and sisters. The Wolf kissed me and asked to be my friend. But unlike Edmund, I knew there were strings attached. I knew all the time. I knew what she wanted. I didn't fall under her spell, like the rest, like magic words and a wand waved over a head.

# PoPPY

I JUMPED IN the Blue Twist. I thought I might want to drown, like Virginia Woolf, even though that wasn't the plan, had never been the plan. But I didn't fill my pockets with stones, so maybe I wasn't truly committed. The water turned me round and round and just when I was about to open my mouth and let it fill my lungs, the river threw me against a dead old tree and I came to a stop.

I crawled out, black dress sticking to my body like glue. I fell on the riverbank and looked up, and never felt so alive.

After that it was just me and the Bell horses and the old Gold Apple Mine by Gold Apple Creek. I slept on hay and ate wild plums. I sang my heart out in the woods, all alone, like Leaf did that one day.

I thought I might be too spoiled and princess-and-the-pea to make it alone, so much had happened since that time I'd run off to my grandpa's cabin. But Wink had faith in me and that gave me faith in myself, and faith was something I never knew I needed until I got it from her.

I caught Wink copying my handwriting once. I figured

she was up to no good, but then, I was never up to any good either, so who was I to judge.

She visited every day, and night, and brought me a fishing rod, and coffee beans, and hardboiled eggs and fruit and sandwiches and cheese and books to read. And I read all her fairy books, every last one, I read them over and over, I read them until they started making sense.

I liked to make people dance. I liked shaking their strings and making them march up and down the stage to my own distinct Poppy tune.

But Wink did too.

More than me, even.

She promised.

She knew where he was. Leaf.

I had to be the wolf, she said. It was her idea, her plan, the unicorn underwear and the kissing contest and the calling her names and the vile Roman Luck house and the making Midnight into a hero. I had to get tied up to the piano and stay there all night and then disappear for a while and then she'd fetch him. She'd fetch him back. And I agreed, I agreed just like that, no hesitation, it was easy for me, as easy as the sun setting, as easy as thunderstorms, and rivers rising, and boys leaving, and two girls reading together in a hayloft.

# Wink

I SPREAD THE rumor that Leaf was finding cures in the Amazon, but he really ran down to California, to the Red Woods. He was living in the forest with some other Heroes, sleeping in tents during the night and fighting the Loggers during the day.

Poppy wanted Leaf. She wanted him so badly that she risked cuddling up to me in the hayloft to find out where he was. The Temptress, gentle words and deliberate gestures. I was supposed to be flattered and shy and overwhelmed, and I was. But not enough.

She left the Temptress behind, eventually. She started using her normal voice. She talked about Leaf, but she talked about other things too. She told me about the Yellows. She told me that she wanted to scream every time her parents called her *their little angel*. She told me that she'd read all the Laura Ingalls Wilder books six times through in secret and she fantasized about cutting off Mary's blond ringlets, right to the skull. She told me that she'd wished she had a younger brother or sister. She told me that she hated the way that everyone at school looked at her like she had all the answers.

She told me how she sometimes stayed up all night just to hear the birds start singing their hearts out come dawn.

# PoᴘᴘY

I HAD THIS idea that maybe they'd all be better off without me anyway, at least for a while. Buttercup and Zoe, and Briggs and Thomas, and Midnight. Like, maybe if I disappeared everyone would be happier, and I'd be happier too, and it wasn't just my self-destructive streak talking. Some people needed to be alone, Thoreau and Emily Dickinson and me. Leaf said that once, and then followed it by saying Thoreau and Emily were better people, way better, even though they were long dead and he'd never met either in person, only read their writing, and yet that still didn't stop him from going on about their supposed shining characters, as compared to me, black and rotten to the core.

When Midnight finally found me at the Gold Apple Mine, I was wearing a kerchief in my hair, a blue one, and washing my clothes in the cold stream, my calves moonlight-white in the water. I know what I looked like, like a wholesome dairymaid or something from a pastel-hued painting, pink cheeks, slightly crooked button nose, working cheerfully in the sunlight. Midnight had been there for a while, I think, just watching me slap a soapy old shirt against a rock.

"You saved my life," he said, when my eyes met his.

"I did," I said back, cool as you please.

And he smiled.

ONCE UPON A time I thought I could change stories, make them go the way I wanted, instead of where they actually went. Leaf warned me against it. He told me I wouldn't find my own story until I stopped messing with everyone else's.

I planned to bring Midnight and the Yellows together at the Roman Luck house. I planned it all along. It was the Final Chapter.

The clues . . . the Yellows would have figured them out soon enough. Together they would have figured it all out, like when Percival Rust gathers the Orphan Bandits and together they crack the code and find the missing girl in *The Grisly Kidnap.*

But the clues were for Midnight, not the Yellows. They were for him alone.

The jasmine. I filled the dip of each candle with the oil, and then, when I lit the wick, the heat spread the smell throughout the room, easy, easy, easy.

I climbed through Midnight's window every day and sprinkled the oil over his bed, easy, easy, easy.

Playing Poppy . . . that was easy too. I'd watched her. I knew her inside and out. I'd read her cover to cover, like *The Thing in the Deep.*

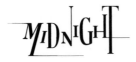

I spent the day with Poppy.

I listened to her.

She listened to me.

I aged about twenty years.

Afterward, I found Wink in the hayloft. Just standing there at the edge of the opening, waiting for me, like she knew.

"You lied," I said, the words out of my mouth before my feet left the ladder. "You plotted with the one person I wanted to leave behind. You manipulated me . . ."

Wink backed up, one step, two.

"You dangled Leaf in front of Poppy and then pushed her over the edge. You let people think she'd *killed* herself. And she almost did. How could you do it? How could you do it, Wink?" I put my hands on the floor and pulled myself inside. I stood. I towered over her, but she didn't flinch this time, didn't turn away. "Did you think that if you created a fairy tale and made all of us play along, made me defeat a monster and become a hero . . . you'd have a happy ending, like a princess in a hayloft story?"

Her red hair hugged her cheeks, long curls covering all the freckles, and the only thing I could see was her damn green eyes, beaming at me, innocent as ever.

She still didn't move. Didn't apologize.

I'd expected lies from Poppy.

But not Wink.

I put my hand to my heart, closed my eyes, tilted my head back . . .

I'd never yelled in my whole life. Never yelled at Alabama, or my parents, not even Mom when she said she was taking my brother and moving to France. Never raised my voice in anger. But I felt it building now. I was going to yell. I was going to yell until my heart burst open, blood spraying everywhere. I was going to yell until there was nothing left inside me, not one damn thing. The sound came, up my throat, buzzing at the back of my teeth . . .

I opened my mouth—

And roared.

It was shaky, and hoarse, and raw.

But it was a roar.

Three seconds and I was done. Spent. I sunk down to the hayloft floor and stayed there.

Wink came over to me after a while. She sat in the hay, knees tucked under her chin, red hair everywhere.

"Can I tell you something?" she asked.

I shrugged, and didn't look at her.

The yelling had left me dark inside.

Empty.

Hollow.

"Pa was tall and lean, with deep brown hair and eyes," she said.

I didn't move. I didn't say anything.

"He was beautiful. I knew this even when I was little. I used to weave my fingers through his hair when he read to me. I'd marvel at the smooth, olive skin of his cheeks next to my own pale, freckled hands. I remember running my thumb over his long eyelashes and liking how they tickled my skin."

She paused.

I sighed.

She kept going.

"Pa first read *The Thing in the Deep* to me when I was

Bee Lee's age. Mim was doing someone's cards and Felix was sleeping next to her and Leaf was off wandering in the woods, which he started doing as soon as he could walk. *Some people are like that*, Pa said. They have the roaming in their blood. He was a roamer at heart too, and came from a long line of them. Bee Lee is the only one of us that looks like him, though Leaf takes after him in all else. *There's no keeping a roamer*, Pa used to whisper in my ear, long before I knew how much he meant it. *You can tie them down, cage them up like a bird, and it will work for a while, but eventually they will break free. And then they'll run until they die.*

"I thought he was the hero. I pictured him in my head when he read the fairy stories to me. He was the adventurer, the explorer, the swashbuckler, the champion. He was Calvino, King of the Thirteenth, and Paolo, the lost heir of World's End. He was Redmayne, singer to the gods, and he was Gabriel the shepherd, and Nathaniel, the builder of cities."

She stopped talking for a long time and just stared at the hay.

Wink was telling the truth. I could feel it.

No fairy tales this time. No lies.

And I was back in, just like that, hook, line, sinker.

"What happened to him?" I asked.

"He left the morning Peach was born. I remember . . . I remember how the mists drifted down from the mountaintops and gave the sun an eerie light. Leaf called it a fairy kind of day and I thought so too. Mim checked herself out of the hospital early and picked us up from Beatrice Comb, who lived off by herself at the foot of Three Death Jack. She watched us sometimes, before she died in her sleep a few winters ago. We got home, and he was gone."

She looked at me, green, green eyes.

"Three months later, I was playing Follow the Screams with Leaf in the woods and I saw something in the Roman Luck house, saw someone moving. I got closer. I peeked in the bay window and there he was, sitting on the green sofa in the music room, reading a newspaper and drinking a cup of coffee, a pile of clothes in the corner, dirty plates on the floor. Pa had been living there, the whole time. *The whole time.* He hadn't even come home to see his new baby."

Long pause.

"And then . . . ?" I asked softly.

"And then he saw me at the window, on my tiptoes, my eyes looking over the sill. He didn't smile at me. Didn't say my name. *Run along.* That's all he said. *Run along.*

"I told Leaf about him. And Leaf told Mim. Pa left after that, left like Roman Luck, gone in the night. Gone for real. Gone for good. Autumn and Martin Lind and the murder, that was storytelling, all storytelling. But I did see a man in the Roman Luck house. I didn't lie. Not about that."

Wink got to her feet, slowly, and walked over to the hayloft opening. I followed. She looked out into the dusky evening light. The twins were on the roof of the farmhouse again, throwing apples at Peach on the ground, who easily dodged them even though she was laughing her head off.

WINK READ THE last chapter of *The Thing in the Deep* that night, and I stayed to watch her do it. I needed her to finish the book. I needed the end. When she was done she closed the book and went over to the far wall. She reached up on her tiptoes and set it on one of the dusty wooden cross-beams.

"I'm not going to read that story again," she said. "I'm done with it, Midnight. Forever."

Dad once told me that the most honorable thing you can do in life is forgive. I didn't believe him at the time, and maybe I still don't. Honor came from defeating foes in battle. From going on long, noble journeys to help those in need. From vanquishing evil and protecting the innocent.

Didn't it?

I left. I walked to the Blue Twist. Alone. I stripped and jumped in naked.

Night sky above.

Cold, dark water below.

I let myself sink down, down, down to the smooth river stones, down into the blackness, until the river ran over my head, and my hair fanned out like flames.

Wink wasn't a villain.

She wasn't a hero.

People aren't just one thing. They never, ever are.

Wink was flesh and blood.

She was bad.

And she was good.

She was real.

And at least I was finally going to get to know her now. The real her.

The real living and breathing and thinking Wink.

# PoPPy

MY PARENTS CAME home from their convention and tromped out to the Gold Apple Mine and demanded I return to civilization, just like they did before when I was out at Grandpa's cabin. But I stood my ground this time, I just kept gutting the trout I'd caught earlier. My mom looked at my bloody hands and flinched, but I was stoic just like Anton Harvey, I was the spitting image. I told my parents I loved them but that living with them was no longer an option, catching fish and sleeping on the ground and being alone a lot was what I'd been built for, this was who I was, and doing the other things, being their little angel, it made me unhappy, and being unhappy made me mean.

My dad muttered something about knowing it all along, I'd had Anton's eyes as a baby, I'd looked right at everyone in the same direct way and my dad *knew* it would come to this . . . though of course he hadn't, the liar. My mom cooed and coaxed and when that didn't work she sadly put her head in her hands, but I'd seen her do the same thing after spending the day with Grandpa, when he was alive, and she always bounced back just fine, so I wasn't worried.

I watched their car as it left, and then stared at the ruts it made in the grass for a while.

They'd be back.

But until then I was going to enjoy the silence, every last peaceful, solitary splash of it.

It was almost sunset. I got my sleeping bag off the wooden mine floor, threw it on the grass, under the stars, so close to the river that I fell asleep with my fingertips in the water.

# MIDNIGHT

I TOLD THE Yellows about Poppy. I told them she was alive and living by herself out at Gold Apple Mine, and that she just wanted to be alone. I told them the letters *were* clues, but they'd been written by Wink, not Poppy—Wink left me clues so I could follow the story to the end, like Thief, when he plays Five Lies, One Truth with the old woman on the Never-Ending Bridge. I told them the séance had been a hoax, and Wink had been behind it all.

The Yellows disbanded.

I think that's what Wink wanted, anyway.

Thomas found another girl to love, a sweet girl named Katie Kelpie who had nice curves and a nice smile and who was always laughing. She drove him around town on the back of her red Vespa and had started to teach him to play the tin whistle so he could join her Irish punk band. Katie talked a mile a minute, only pausing long enough to gaze up at Thomas and make sure he was happy, and he usually was.

I sometimes saw Buttercup and Zoe in the cemetery when I walked into town, taking gravestone rubbings and whispering in each other's ears, like always, like nothing was missing.

Briggs.

I ran into him in the woods. It was a windy day, almost dusk. He was sitting beside a green tent and small fire, staring into space.

"If being alone out in nature is good enough for Poppy, it's good enough for me," he said, after a while.

I just nodded.

"She never loved us, you know. Not any of us."

I nodded again. "How long you plan on being out here in the woods, Briggs?"

He shrugged. "As long as it takes."

I left him by his fire.

I went over to the Bell farm and walked right through the kitchen door, no knocking, because that's how things stood now. Mim was melting something over the stove, something that smelled like butter and honey and roses. Her red hair was tied back with a green scarf, and the sleeves of her black shirt were rolled up to her freckled elbows.

"Hold out your hand," she said without looking up.

I did. She dropped a creamy dollop in the middle of my palm.

"It's shea butter dream cream. It helps you sleep."

I rubbed my hands together. "It smells good. What will it make me dream?"

Mim didn't answer but she flashed me a mysterious smile over her shoulder. And she looked so much like Wink when she did it that I got goose bumps.

"It's so quiet," I said. "Where is everyone?"

"Felix saw that white deer this morning and they all ran off to follow him. Wink packed a picnic for the Orphans, so they could be a while."

I sat down at the table. There was a freshly shelled bowl of sugar snap peas and I picked up a handful of the little green guys and put them in my mouth.

Mim started filling clear glass jars with the dream balm, one careful teaspoon at a time. She paused for a second, hands on her hips. She turned away from the counter, leaned across the table, and moved the bowl of peas out of the way.

"I'm going to read the cards for you, Midnight."

"All right," I said.

"No, I'm going to read *Wink's* cards for you."

That got me. "But Wink told me that you won't read your kids' cards anymore, ever since you read Bee Lee's once and learned she was going to die young."

Mim looked at me and frowned, deep, lips tucking in at the corners. "Those weren't Bee Lee's cards. They were Wink's."

My heart stopped beating.

It did.

I put my palm to my chest and pushed in.

"I never told her," Mim said. "But she started reading cards at twelve, and she learned it for herself. I thought knowing her future might help. Might make her embrace life, live it to the fullest. I was wrong. And then her father up and left too, and they were so close."

I pressed harder, my whole hand into my chest.

"I don't believe in tarot," I said. "I don't believe in fortune-telling."

She pulled the cards out anyway, a quick tug of the hidden pocket. She laid them on the table.

A skeleton.

A dead man pierced with swords.

A cloaked figure, five gold goblets.

Two dogs howling at the moon.

A heart with three daggers, sunk to the hilt.

"Yes," Mim said quietly.

I didn't know what the cards meant, or what Mim saw in them, but there was sadness blazing in her Wink-green eyes.

"The cards could be wrong," I said.

"Maybe." Mim swept up the cards with one hand and put them back in her pocket. She turned to the glass jars and the dream balm, paused, and then looked at me over her shoulder. "Right or wrong, Wink believes them. And that changes everything."

I FOUND WINK in the hayloft. The Orphans were put to bed at midnight and then it was just the two of us and a blanket on the hay and the moon shining in. We talked for hours. All truth, no fairy tales.

I was almost asleep when she kissed me. She kissed my neck and my chin and my ears and everything in between. She unbuttoned my shirt and I unbuttoned her strawberry overalls. She wrapped her bare arms around me and gripped my back, hard, and I swear I could feel her freckles pressing into my skin, every last one of them.

She didn't arch her spine or flip her hair.

I pulled away. I looked at her, and she smiled. She smiled right *into* me—I felt it echo in my ribs, like a shout, like a deep, deep sigh.

Her body curved into mine, chest to chest, my face in her hair.

"Wink," I whispered, sometime close to dawn, everything quiet but the sky still black. *"Wink."*

I put my palm against her heart and waited for it to beat. And beat. And beat.

She squirmed and looked up at me. And I could see it in her eyes. She knew.

"Mim read my cards for you."

I nodded.

I felt her shrug, her skin moving against mine.

"My heart might have two billion beats left in it, or two hundred." She sighed. "But it doesn't matter that much. It doesn't. I used to think that I needed to be part of a story, a *big story*, one with trials and villains and temptations and rewards. That's how I would conquer it, conquer *death*."

She sighed again, and nestled closer into me. "All that matters, in the end, is the little things. The way Mim says my name to wake me up in the morning. The way Bee's hand feels in mine. The way the sun cast my shadow across the yard yesterday. The way your cheeks flush when we kiss. The smell of hay and the taste of strawberries and the feel of fresh black dirt between my toes. This is what matters, Midnight."

I SAW THE white stag on the way home. He was standing by the apple trees, gleaming like he was made of starlight. He took one long look at me and then bounded off into the dark.

I closed my eyes and made a wish.

# WINK

THE END OF the summer.

The end of this story.

I kept my promise to Poppy.

I sent for Leaf.

I mailed a letter west, to California, to a cabin in the Red Woods.

Leaf followed his own beat and listened to no one. I didn't know if my letter would work. Part of me wished I could ask the birds to fetch him, snatch him in their claws and carry him through the sky like Andrew in *The Raven War*. But part of me also hoped that Leaf would just come back on his own, because I asked him to.

The coyote knew he'd returned before I did. I saw him at the edge of the forest, watching the Roman Luck path. Leaf smiled when he saw the both of us waiting for him, the coyote and me.

Later, after he'd hugged Mim and Bee Lee and let Felix introduce his girlfriend and played Follow the Screams with the twins and Peach . . . he went to her. I left them alone for a while, but in the end I had to see. I snuck over to the Gold

Apple Mine, hiding in the shadows like I used to. They were there, sitting by the creek, watching the setting sun, shoulder to shoulder, blond and red.

# POPPY

LEAF.

"So this is how you live now?" he asked.

I felt his eyes on me, on my back, cutting through my clothes, scorching my skin.

I looked at him over my shoulder. He was leaning against the doorframe of the old Gold Apple Mine, red hair and freckles and bony limbs, watching me start a fire. I smiled, a real Poppy smile, not any of those fake smiles I'd been using for so many years.

"Yes," I said. "I figured it out. I figured myself out."

Leaf laughed. He *laughed*, deep and bright, like he'd never done before, not with me anyway.

"Prove it," he said.

And I did.

# MIDNIGHT

I WAS READING by the apple trees, bare feet in the green grass, when I heard the rumble. I looked up. Black clouds rolling in.

The hayloft was the place for thunderstorms. Wink and I liked to listen to the rain beat on the roof, watch lightning buzz across the sky.

I took my time, walking over to the barn, stopping to watch the clouds, letting the thunder boom straight into my heart.

I climbed up the ladder, stuck my head through the opening, and there she was, sitting on the hay, eating strawberries from a green bowl with one hand, and turning the pages of a book with the other. She was alone. The Orphans must have been off in the woods, playing one of their Orphan games.

I opened my mouth to call out to her—

And I saw the cover of the book.

A boy with a sword at his side. Standing on a hill. Facing a dark, stone castle. Grim-looking mountains in the background.

I closed my eyes.

Opened them.

I climbed back down the ladder, quiet.

I walked home.

I went straight up to the attic.

"Dad?"

"Yes?"

"I want to fly to France to see Mom and Alabama."

He looked up. He didn't smile, but his eyes crinkled at the corners. "Okay," he said.

"And I want you to come with."

"Okay," he said again, just like that.

FRANCE.

I drank café au laits. I climbed castles. I walked in French moonlight along French riverbanks. I spent long afternoons with Mom and Alabama, sunshine and lavender-scented breezes and distant church bells and talking about Mom's book.

I hadn't said good-bye to Wink. Hadn't written her a letter. Hadn't called.

Silence.

I told Alabama. I told him everything. All of it. I wasn't looking for his advice. I just wanted to share, like brothers do.

We sat in the courtyard behind our ancient stone house

at the edge of Lourmarin. Mom was inside writing and Dad was at a book auction in Avignon. They went their separate ways during the day, but later . . . later we would all have a lazy al fresco dinner in the town square, and then a long walk together come twilight.

Alabama reached his brown arms up and tied his straight hair back, away from his face.

I thought about how little I looked like him. But I didn't mind this time.

I told Alabama about my summer, about the Roman Luck house, the unforgivables, the tarot cards, *The Thing in the Deep*, and Wink. Wink, Wink, Wink. He didn't say a word. Not until the very end.

His black eyes met mine. "You should have said good-bye."

"I know."

He didn't say anything else for a while. We listened to the birds singing in the four nearby lemon trees, and drank espresso from two small, fat brown cups.

Eventually my brother gave a long, low whistle and shook his head. "Right now? That red-haired girl needs her fairy tales. You just gotta let her be, Midnight."

I let that sink in. "Like how you're just letting Talley Jasper be, you mean?"

Alabama grinned, slow and easy. "Exactly. We've got time, brother. We've got all the time in the world."

I SAW A girl who looked like Wink that night. She was small, and her long hair was straight, but red. Red, red, red. She was reading a book while walking two little black dogs in the trees near the chateau, at the edge of Lourmarin. It was dusk.

I pictured Wink in the girl's black boots and saffron-yellow dress. I pictured Wink in the woods, blue shadows, gray fog, dark sky. The two dogs became the Witch Wolves, following at her heels, snarling and snapping at the air.

I closed my eyes . . .

And I was there suddenly, back in the Roman Luck woods.

Wink.

I wove my hands into her hair, and felt the thick curls tugging my fingers apart. The wolves growled, but I ignored them.

Wink kissed the inside of my wrists, right, then left.

I sighed.

She put her hand on my heart.

The wolves began to howl.

She looked up at me, green, green eyes.

*"Good-bye, Midnight,"* she said. *"Good-bye for now."*

And then she and her wolves disappeared into the fog, going, going, gone.

I opened my eyes.

The French girl was watching me, watching as I just stood

there in the trees with my eyes shut, dreaming about a red-haired girl a million miles away.

She smiled at me.

I smiled back.

EVERY STORY NEEDS a Hero.

The Hero of this story sat in a hayloft, surrounded by books. She pointed her pointy chin at the rafters and shouted out into the night. Her freckles danced across her cheeks like the stars danced across the sky.

The Hero found the boy in the woods. He had dark hair and two different-colored eyes. One blue, one green.

The Hero thought the boy might be the Villain.

Every story needs a Villain.

But . . .

But the boy was sitting by a small fire, and there was a lost look in his blue and green eyes.

The boy reminded the Hero of Thief . . . Thief, who used to sit beside his small fire and sing the old songs to keep his loneliness at bay.

The Hero sat down beside the boy. He started talking about

his true love, the golden-haired girl he'd lost to a valiant warrior named the Red Knight.

The Hero had lost her true love too. He ran off in the night. He crossed an ocean and went to live in a place with trickster cats and enchanted princes and wives hung on walls by blue-bearded men.

The Hero talked to the boy all night long. They shared a crisp red apple and a mug of golden milk and a piece of gingerbread. And then, when dawn came, the boy packed up his tent, gave the Hero a smile—a solid, true one—and went home.

The Hero stood alone in the forest, red hair flowing down her back.

She held out her arms and felt the plump, sunrise breeze blow across her skin.

The Hero suddenly knew that this story wouldn't be like all the other stories. There wouldn't be swords, or monsters, or trials. There wouldn't be riddles, or revenge, or resurrections.

But there would be redemption.

And love.

And life.

And ever after.

## Acknowledgments

Jessica Garrison. Editor, friend.

Everyone at Dial and Penguin, especially Bri Lockhart, Kristin Smith, and Colleen Conway.

My inimitable agent, Joanna Volpe. Thanks for the tarot in New Orleans, and for liking the gypsy romp.

Klindt's Booksellers.

Katharine Mary Briggs, queen of the fairy tales.

Mandy Buehrlen.

Kenny Brechner.

Nova Ren Suma.

Victoria Scott, for the circle of fire.

Megan Shepherd—what would I do without you?

Kendare Blake, for calling me the kitchen witch.

Alistair Cairns and Kelly Cannon-Miller, for skull-watching.

The Hicks kids.

Dad.

Nate.

## About the Author

**APRIL GENEVIEVE TUCHOLKE** is the critically acclaimed author of *Between the Devil and the Deep Blue Sea* and *Between the Spark and the Burn* and curated the horror/thriller anthology *Slasher Girls & Monster Boys*. April has lived in many places around the world. She currently resides in Oregon with her husband.